Crossed Wires
Life's Outtakes – Year 8

52 Humorous and Inspirational Short Stories

By
Daris Howard

A collection of stories, humorous anecdotes, thoughts, and tidbits of wisdom from the popular newspaper column.

Publishing Inspiration

Crossed Wires

Life's Outtakes - Year 8

52 Humorous and Inspirational Short Stories

By

Daris W. Howard

A collection of stories, humorous anecdotes, thoughts, and tidbits of wisdom from the newspaper column

Life's Outtakes.

ISBN-10: 1629860069
ISBN-13: 978-1629860060

www.publishinginspiration.com

Publishing Date: July 2015

Publishing Inspiration LLC

Table of Contents

Dear Reader,

People often ask me if my stories are true. Though I must admit that I tend to take a bit of literary license in my writing, each story is based on an actual event. Sometimes the stranger stories are the ones that are stretched the least. As people often say, truth is stranger than fiction.

I also want to note that some of the names have been changed to protect the anonymity of the individuals.

Daris Howard

Ordering American Food in Peru

I had ordered all sorts of food in Peru. I had tried chicken with a side of beans, beef with a side of beans, alpaca with a side of beans, and beans with a side of beans. I was starting to feel like a human bean and decided it was time to see if I could find some American food. I expressed my feelings to others in our group, and they agreed.

We hunted all over Cuzco. Thankfully, most of the restaurants post their menus on their front window, and many of those are listed in both Spanish and in English.

We hunted for a long time, and the best we found was a pizza place. We were excited until we looked at the menu. The bread was more of a taco, and there were pizzas with beans and cheese; beans, rice, and cheese; and three different kinds of beans with cheese.

"Bean pizza?" I asked my colleagues.

One of them shrugged. "It was bound to happen."

In all of our searching that night we didn't find anything, and eventually we had to settle for the regular fare. That week we traveled over much of Peru, and one night we pulled into our hotel in a small town named Yucay. Right next to our hotel was a restaurant with a sign written in both English and Spanish. The sign read, "Peruvian and American Food."

We couldn't believe our luck. We looked at the menu, and it had line after line of the regular Peruvian foods. But then there was the "American" section. Underneath it there was a single item, and it plainly read, "Hamburger and fries with side salad."

I questioned the waiter as to whether this truly was an American hamburger and fries. He beamed proudly. "Of course. Our cook go America and learn cook American food. He say nothing more American than hamburger and fries."

I couldn't believe it, an American hamburger right there in

one of the tiniest Peruvian towns we had been in. I placed my order and waited with great anticipation. The others in our group were much more skeptical.

"Do you trust them when they only have one American item?" one in our group asked.

"I'm sure they are just trying to do one thing well," I replied.

The rest of our group all ended up ordering something they were more sure about, and I couldn't blame them. I had had a bad experience once ordering tuna and asking for it to be served on bread with mayonnaise, only to find out tuna was the fruit of a cactus.

But, finally, the moment arrived. The fries were there. They were just a potato cut into strips and cooked in an oven. They might have been the slightest bit brown, definitely not fries by American standards.

But the hamburger was even more interesting. There was a hamburger patty with cheese melting on it, but there was no bun. The "side salad" was a nice stack of lettuce, a big slice of tomato, and a few pickles — basically all the fixings for a hamburger, but without the bun. And, of course, beside them was an order of beans.

When I asked the waiter about the bun, he looked confused. "Wait minute," he said, disappearing into the kitchen. When he came back he said, "Cook say, American side order of decorative roll is extra."

I realized that when the cook had gone to America, he had misunderstood what the bun was for. In Peru, bread is served before the meal as a precursor to the main dish. Then, as the meal comes, the waiter clears the bread away. It seems it is inappropriate to eat bread with the main dish. Perhaps it is an insult to the chef if it is deemed necessary to the meal.

"You like side dish of decorative roll?" the waiter asked.

I shook my head, not wanting to offend the cook. "No, thanks."

I added beans to my hamburger patty, put the side salad on top, and ate it with a fork.

Gaining Strength to Endure

I had a knee replacement a couple of weeks ago. Usually a person needs a knee replacement when they are getting old and their body is wearing out, but mine wasn't because of age. Mine was due to a major athletic accident thirty years ago.

When I got my tonsils out at forty-five years old, the doctor told me it would be hard on me because I was so old. It was interesting to have the knee doctor tell me I would struggle with knee surgery because I was so young.

"Oh, you should come through the surgery with flying colors," he said. "But the therapy is going to be much harder on you. Muscles and ligaments at your age won't be as flexible and will mend faster, making therapy much harder than if you were older. You will have to work harder and endure more pain so you can get back your full range of motion and not walk with a limp the rest of your life. Do you feel up to it?"

I remembered back when I had first had my athletic accident. It was severe. I tore just about every ligament away from the bone all the way from my hip to my ankle. I had bolts, staples, and pins throughout most of my leg. Then, after the surgery, I had some complications from infections and anesthesia. I nearly had to have my leg amputated to save my life.

When I was finally stabilized, my dream of going to the Olympics was gone. Instead, the doctor informed me that it might be all I could do to be able to walk again.

He said, "It will depend upon you and how much you can endure in physical therapy."

After almost eight weeks the cast came off, and I found my leg had almost no muscle at all. It had atrophied and locked into the slightly bent position of the cast. I can remember that, after scratching and scratching, I finally attempted my first step. I fell

3

onto my crutches, dizzy with pain, and the doctor and the nurse kept me from tipping over.

I can well remember that first physical therapy session when my leg felt like a solid board, and the different things the therapist was doing felt like he was trying to break that board. The pain was excruciating, and I doubted whether I could bear it.

After I had had about a half hour of this, a little six-year-old girl was carried in by her father and set on the therapy table next to me. She had horrible arthritis and was all curled up in a fetal position. Her father left the room, unable to watch his daughter struggle through the pain.

I watched as a therapist started working her arms and legs. The tears rolled down her face, and once in a while she would scream. But then she would always smile and tell them she could endure it, and asked them to continue.

At one point, everyone left the two of us alone to rest for a brief time, and I asked her how she learned to be so brave. She smiled through all of her pain as she answered, "I want to be a normal girl, so I come here twice each week. After they work with me, I can walk and use my arms for a few days. I do the therapy so I can be like everyone else."

As the therapists came back and started working with the two of us, the little girl's courage gave me courage, and I endured more than I ever thought possible. As we finished up, I watched the little girl walk from the therapy room holding her father's hand. She stopped at the door, turned, smiled, and waved.

"Good luck," she called to me. I smiled and waved back, and I knew I had found the courage I needed. I would walk again.

So, as the doctor asked me if I would be able to deal with the therapy for my knee replacement, I thought of the little girl, and I smiled. "Yes, I will be able to do it."

Most of my college students are bright, fun to teach, and hard working. But each semester I get interesting letters, emails, and phone calls from a few students. I save these, and, occasionally, I compile them into a column. The last couple of years I have shared some of these, and, with school just starting, I thought I'd share a few more. I don't think any of these comments need any explanation, other than to say that I changed or removed any names for anonymity. Also, I pared down a few of them a bit.

I want you to know that the fact that I am failing your class isn't a reflection on my math skills. I am actually really good at math. I have just been busy. I want you to know that I am actually doing worse in my other classes.

Hey, Professor Howard, I'm sorry I've been missing so many classes. I haven't been feeling well, and my doctor has needed me a couple of times over the past week and a half.

I have a C overall in your class on the tests and projects. I also have a B on my homework. My question is this, when you take the B on my homework and average it with the C I already have, will that raise me to an A in the class?

I came to your office to get help on the Excel spreadsheet. You walked me through it step by step, and it looked good, but when I went home to do it, it didn't work again. Is there something I am missing?

I was checking my grades online and noticed that I received a zero for both my exam review and my 4c project. I turned them in with everyone else, so I was wondering why I didn't get any of the points for these assignments. When I got them back, you had written a note saying there was no name so you didn't know who to give points to. Even if I forgot my name, shouldn't you have at least given me some points?

I wasn't in class on Friday and there was an attendance quiz. How do I make up points for an attendance quiz for a day I wasn't in class?

I'm writing because I just saw my final grade and I am not happy. I basically had this math in high school and was mad that I had to take it again, so I decided that I was not going to waste my time coming to class, doing homework and projects, or anything else since I already knew it. I was sure I could get enough points on the tests to pass the class and wouldn't need points from the other stuff. But you write your tests weird, or something, because I didn't know what the questions were about and didn't do well on any of them. And now my grade says I failed and that makes me mad. How can I fail a class on material that I already know? I need you to let me know what you are going to do so I pass. Please write back right away.

I saw the button for the online quiz we were supposed to take, so I clicked on it to see what would happen. It took me to the quiz, but I wasn't ready, so I got out of it and now it has locked me out because it says I already attempted it. I didn't really attempt it. I just clicked on the button that took me into it. Can you fix that for me?

I am sorry, but I won't be able to attend class today. I got a bad case of food poisoning. My roommate thinks he can cook, but he can't.

How the West Was to One

I was a sophomore in high school, and it was the first day of the school year. There was a new boy, Skip, who was in my athletic training class. He was big, muscular, and showed a lot of athletic ability. But I had never seen anyone that seemed so timid. In fact, it was more than timidity; he was just plain strange.

We started out the class by lifting weights. Skip watched the weight room door nervously. If it ever started to open, he would dash around behind the weight machine and peer cautiously out from behind it. Once the person who had opened the door had entered the room, he would slowly come out and go back to lifting weights.

The first time seemed like a coincidence, but after this had happened a few times, everyone realized it wasn't. Finally, after a half dozen episodes of this, curiosity got the better of Lenny, and he walked over to Skip.

"Hey, you new here or what?" Lenny asked.

Skip nodded. "Just moved here yesterday from the East coast."

The rest of us gathered around. "Are you feeling all right?" Lenny asked.

Skip looked at us and shrugged. "Sure. Why wouldn't I be?"

Just then Coach stepped into the room, and Skip darted around behind the weight machine. "Hey, is this a speech class?" Coach bellowed. "I thought I sent you in here to lift weights. Well, if you aren't going to do that, you can all head out to the track and run a mile." Everyone groaned. "And if I catch anybody walking," Coach continued, "it will be two miles tomorrow."

Coach turned and headed back to his office, and Skip came out from behind the weight machine. "You don't have to be scared of Coach," Lenny said to him. "He's got a big bark, but he's okay."

7

"What makes you think I'm scared of him?" Skip asked.

We all just looked at each other, and Lenny shrugged. We made our way through the gym, heading on our way out to the track. As we reached the outside door, Skip paused. He warily looked out as the rest of us continued on to the track. Suddenly, Skip took off out the door, running full speed past us. When he reached the track, he threw himself under the bleachers.

Lenny leaned over to me and whispered. "I don't know about you, but this guy is freaking me out."

When the rest of us reached the track, we started jogging. As we passed the bleachers where Skip was, he nervously joined us, trying to keep right in the middle of the main group. As we finished our mile, he quickly hid under the bleachers again. Lenny couldn't stand it anymore.

"What are you doing?" he yelled at Skip.

"Hiding from the Indians," Skip said.

"What Indians?" Lenny asked.

"You know, the ones that will attack and . . . " Suddenly Skip paused. He slowly came out from his hiding place and looked at us. "Aren't you guys scared?"

"Scared of what?" Lenny asked.

"Well, I've seen Western movies where Indians came and attacked and . . . " He stopped again. "Do Indians not do that any more?"

"I don't know," Lenny said. "Let's ask David. He's an Indian." Lenny then turned to David Bearclaw. "David, do you plan to attack us?"

David laughed. "Only if you steal my brownie from my lunch tray again like you did today."

Skip smiled an embarrassed smile. "I guess the real danger is only in being afraid of what we don't understand."

Those Annoying Things in Life

You know, sometimes little things can be so annoying. Take, for example, the day I went to help an old friend. Winter was coming on, and he asked me to pack insulation underneath his trailer house, especially around the water pipes. The winter before had been very cold, and more than once the water pipes under his house had frozen. I had spent many hours that winter running heaters under his trailer to thaw the pipes to get the water flowing again. We hoped to get enough insulation tucked around the pipes so that we wouldn't face the same problem in the upcoming winter.

So after work one evening, I started by trying to take off the trailer skirting on the front of his house. I loosened some and then reached a point where it went behind the stairs that led to the front door. I really didn't want to take the stairs off since I knew that would be a big job.

I tried to pry the stairs out just enough so that I could get the skirting off, but no matter how I tried, I couldn't get it off with the stairs in the way. That was when I considered how annoying little things can be, and resigned myself to the fact that I had no other option but to remove the stairs.

It took a good hour to get them loose, but I was finally able to move them out about a foot. Again I tried to get the skirting off, but I still needed more room. I pulled and tugged and finally moved the stairs out another foot. I still couldn't get the skirting off. Finally, in frustration, I dragged the stairs out inch by inch until they were about six feet from the trailer. I knew they definitely couldn't be in the way there.

I got the skirting off and climbed under the trailer house. I was exasperated to find that the pipe ran to the back of the trailer and that it was really the back skirting I needed to take off.

Sometimes little things can be so annoying.

I started the same process on the back of the house and eventually had to move the back stairs. Finally, with everything clear, I was able to climb in to where I could tuck insulation up around the pipes. Carefully I put it all along underneath them, stapling it to the cross beams as I went. It was filthy, hot work. By the time I finished with the insulation, I was itchy and sweaty, and the sun was going down fast.

My throat was parched and cracked, and I desperately needed water, but it was almost impossible to get into the trailer to a faucet where I could get a drink. So I worked as fast as I could to get the back skirting in place. Once I had it where it needed to be, I tugged and pulled and pushed to get the back stairs against the trailer.

Just as the darkness settled in, they were nailed tightly into position, and I could get some water. I was feeling slightly dizzy as I made my way to the kitchen. I drank two full glasses of water and then slowly sipped a third.

My old friend invited me to take a break and sit down for a visit. I filled one more glass of water and accepted his invitation. After we visited for a while, I figured I should be getting home to my own family.

It wasn't until I walked out the front door and face-planted into the dirt that I remembered I had forgotten to put the front stairs back on.

Sometimes little things can be so annoying.

Different Generations

It was harvest time, and Dolores struggled to feel that she was of any value. From the time she was a young married bride, she had worked beside her husband in the fields. She had been as proficient at running a horse team as any man. Later, as times changed, she learned to work tractors, trucks, and every other kind of farm equipment.

But things continued to change, and as she grew older, she found herself being replaced, first by her sons and daughters, and then by her grandchildren. They felt she was too old to be working in the fields, and she had to admit that some of the fancy, modern equipment seemed strange.

Every time she would try to find a place to work in the cellars, in the fields, or on the equipment, one of her grandchildren would come along and say, "It's okay, Grandma, I'll do that."

Finally she retreated to the farmhouse where her son lived. It was, in many ways, the command and control center for the harvest activities. Though it wouldn't be the physical, active work she had always done, she knew she could at least find some usefulness there.

She baked bread, pies, and cookies, and cooked mounds of mashed potatoes and pots of roast beef. At mealtime the workers would descend on the kitchen and wolf down the meals, grateful for the good food. That helped her feel better, but still she wished she could do more.

That was when she noticed the piles of laundry. With the hard, dirty work, and everyone out in the fields, the laundry was stacking up. She knew she could do that. She washed load after load. As the first loads started coming out of the dryer, she started folding the clothes. That was when she noticed something else she could do.

Many of her grandchildren's jeans were holey and frayed. She had grown up during the depression, and if there was one thing she knew how to do, it was to patch worn-out jeans. She stacked everything that needed patching into one pile. She was amazed at how many there were.

She had to prepare another meal before she could start the mending, but she kept her plans a secret so she could surprise her grandchildren once all of their clothes were done.

Finally came the time she could sit down and start her work. She worked efficiently, day after day, and by the time the harvest was over, she had put the last patch on the final pair of jeans. She could hardly wait to show everyone her fine work.

When she presented her grandchildren with their repaired jeans, their reaction and the expression of horror on their faces was unexpected. One grandson expressed their thoughts. "Ahhh, Grandma!" he said. "You have ruined our jeans!"

"What do you mean?" Dolores asked. "They were full of holes and all frayed, and I patched them."

"But, Grandma," the grandson said, "we paid hundreds of dollars to buy them that way."

"A store sold you clothes that were torn and full of holes?" Dolores asked. "They should be ashamed of themselves for selling such poor quality goods."

Her grandchildren just rolled their eyes, and she knew she was missing something. But that night, as she was about to head back to her own home, her grandchildren gathered around her. "Grandma," her grandson said, "we just wanted to thank you for your love and for working so hard to patch our jeans."

She smiled. "I hope it makes them nicer to wear."

Her grandson smiled back at her. "Oh, I'm not sure we'll wear them that much except for farm work. But we'll keep them as a reminder of you and a reminder to make sure our school clothes aren't in the laundry at harvest time."

They all then gave her a hug, and she felt happy, even though she knew she would never understand the younger generation.

We Are All in This Together

Liza stared at the young man, Mr. Winthrop, who stood at her door. The fear and concern showed in his face. "Please?" he begged. "Please, won't you come? I'm afraid my wife and baby will die without your help."

Liza had grown up in the city and was highly educated and well-trained as a midwife. But she fell in love with a man who took her far away to the rugged west. When her husband died, Liza found herself trying to run her farm and take care of her eight children while still using her midwifery skills to help others. But too often she was busy helping others when she needed to be directing her sons in the harvest. Between that and people not paying her for the help delivering the babies, she lost her farm.

She moved to a new community and found a rundown farm. It had a small dilapidated cabin. She and her children worked hard to fix up the cabin and plant the farm. But now it was harvest time again, and the cold days were approaching. If they didn't get the beet crop harvested, she would never be able to make the farm payments.

But with all of these worries, the thought of the young mother trying to give birth and possibly losing her life became Liza's overriding concern.

She turned to her oldest son. "David, Mr. Winthrop's horses are exhausted. Please unhitch them and hitch ours to his wagon while I get my things ready to go."

By the time she had everything packed, the wagon was ready. As she climbed up beside Mr. Winthrop, she took David's hand. "Take care of things here, and try to harvest what you can."

David nodded. "We'll be okay, Mother."

Mr. Winthrop pushed the horses hard, but it was still a few hours before they arrived at his home. When Liza entered the room where Mrs. Winthrop was laboring to give birth to the baby, she could tell immediately that the situation was desperate. The additional time it had taken for her to get there had stressed both the mother and the baby.

She worked skillfully and quickly, and within an hour, the baby was born. But the ordeal was a long way from being over. The baby's heartbeat was erratic, and the mother was barely conscious. Liza continued to work to stabilize both of them.

For many days Liza worked to help the young mother and the baby. Other women came to help, and Liza directed their combined efforts. Mr. Winthrop did everything she asked, and he was there with his wife, helping Liza during many sleepless nights.

It was almost a full week before Liza felt everything was all right, and she knew that the next day she would finally be able to return home. But each night she had stayed there, the weather had grown a little colder. And that last night the temperature dropped so low she knew the beets in the ground would be frozen.

The next day, as Mr. Winthrop hitched the team to take her home, she could barely hold back the tears. It was a long ride home as she wondered if she would have to move and start over again. But as they finally turned onto the road on her farm, to her surprise, she saw empty row after empty row of already harvested beets.

When they pulled into the yard, her children ran to greet her. "David, how did you get the beets all harvested?" she asked.

He just laughed. "It wasn't just us. The whole community came."

Mr. Winthrop smiled at her. "That's the way it is here. When you are helping someone else, others are there to help you."

And this time Liza could not stop her tears from coming, because for the first time in a long time, she knew what it felt like to be part of a truly caring community.

For Whom the Horn Blows

I had been working as a landscape laborer, digging ditches, laying sod, and all sorts of physical labor. But as school started in the fall, the cold set in, and there was very little of that type of work to be had. I checked the employment board at the university twice each day trying to be the first in line for any new job that might open.

I did odd jobs of all kinds and continued to look for more steady work. Then, finally, I saw a posting for someone to drive a mail truck around campus. I hurried and filled out the application, and soon had the job.

Each afternoon at one o'clock, after I finished my classes, I would bike over to the campus mail center. Afternoon classes were still in full swing, and it was often a slow drive to the buildings in the center of campus since I had to make my way down busy sidewalks.

I drove the last mail run of the day, and I collected and dropped off mail at every building's mail room. Seldom did I have to sort the mail into the separate mailboxes, as that was someone else's job. But once in a while, when we were shorthanded, I would receive a sorting assignment in a few of the buildings.

One day, a few of our mail sorters had the flu, and everyone needed to do extra work. In the center of campus the three biggest and busiest buildings were laid out in a triangle, and it was in them that I was assigned to sort the mail after I dropped it off. I decided, for efficiency, to haul the bins of mail from the truck into each building and then work my way back, sorting as I went.

I had just finished hauling the mail to the last of the three buildings when a vehicle's horn started to blare. It was so loud I could hear it clear into the mail room in the center of the building, and its tone was grating and obnoxious. The horn blared the whole time I sorted, and I couldn't believe its owner didn't get it stopped. As I stepped from the building, the horn was so loud that I knew it had to be heard all over the campus. I quickly sorted the mail in the next two buildings with the horn blaring the whole time. I finally finished and headed back to my truck.

As I approached it, to my dismay, I found it surrounded by hundreds of people, and, worst of all, it had its horn stuck on. Curious students were leaning out the windows of all of the surrounding buildings. Half a dozen campus security cars were there, and the officers were trying to control the crowd and deal with the situation. The police had set up temporary barricades around my truck to keep back those who were agitated and threatening harm to it. People were yelling and waving their arms, trying to be understood above the noise.

I worked my way through the crowd and reached the police barricade. The officer there saw the mail bins I carried and let me through. When the officer who was trying to break into my truck saw me, he moved aside, and I unlocked it. I popped the hood and quickly pulled a wire from the horn.

Suddenly, everything was quiet. I turned with a sheepish grin to face the crowd. The students, who were happy to miss class, were laughing, but the professors, whose classes the noise had disrupted, looked like they wanted my blood.

I saw one professor I knew. Trying to diffuse the situation, I joked to him, "I was wondering who it was who let his horn blare like that."

Before he turned to go back to salvage what he could of his class, he glared at me and replied, "Well, I guess now we all know who the idiot is, don't we?"

Loading Pigs

Early one spring, my father purchased a cute little weaner pig for us to raise. To me fell the assignment to feed it. When it was small, it was fun to haul the food scraps, garden weeds, and sour milk to it. The little pig would climb right into the trough with his food. He would root through it to eat the choicest bits first.

I would laugh at his antics as he would bite into something that was less desirable. He would shake his head and oink his displeasure. When he was full and happy, he would come to me and nuzzle me, begging for treats.

But as the summer progressed, he grew at an average of five pounds per day, and he was no longer cute. By the time he was over four hundred pounds, he no longer begged for his treats, but knocked me down if I withheld them.

When fall came and he was more than five hundred pounds, my father decided it was time that the pig moved on. We put the cattle rack on our old pickup, and my father backed it up to the pig's pen so we could load him.

We set up the ramp into the pickup, and, when my father moved into position to help me load the pig, I said, "It's okay, Dad, I can do it."

He smiled and left me to accomplish what I thought would be an easy job. I was, after all, twelve years old and an expert cow herder. How different could it be for a pig — especially just one?

I got behind the pig and started shooing him toward the ramp. He paid no attention to me, so I gave his rump a swat. He took off toward the ramp and then ran a circle around me.

I tried again. I got behind him and moved slowly toward him. He again moved toward the ramp, but as before, at the last minute he turned. He attempted to run around me, but I was ready this time. I jumped in his path, yelling and waving my arms. He plowed through me like wasn't even there.

I picked myself up and brushed the hoofprints from my clothes. I was mad now. Again I moved him toward the ramp and once more he turned. But I didn't plan to let him plow me over. I threw myself at him. But 100 pounds does not fare too well against 500. I was like a small compact car in the path of a freight train.

He hit me hard, and I felt the wind go out of me, but I held on. I had my arms wrapped around his neck and one leg over his back. He didn't seem to like the idea of being ham-pered in his escape. He took off at full speed, running circles around his pen, squealing as he went.

I was afraid that if I fell off he would trample me, so I held on tight, and away we raced in a literal competition to bring home the bacon. After a few rounds, he widened his circle and took me under a low rafter that caught me hard in the head, knocking me to the ground.

As I slowly pulled myself together and stood up, I saw an old neighbor standing there, grinning. "Were you planning on loading that pig or entering him as a steed in a bacon derby?"

"Son," he continued. "That pig outweighs you by five times. You can't beat him by strength. Do you want to know how to load him?" I nodded, so he handed me a bucket. "Take this and put it over his head. He will try to back out of it. You just keep moving forward and back him into the truck."

I stuck the bucket over the pig's head, and, sure enough, he backed away. I stepped with him, and he kept backing. I moved right or left to steer him as needed. He loaded into the truck with barely a hitch, and I latched the door.

My old neighbor grinned. "You've really got to be smarter than the pig."

Missing a Halloween Party

As school was ending on Friday, Lenny stopped by my locker to see me. "Do you want to join us for some Halloween fun tomorrow?"

"What are you going to do?" I asked.

"We're going to help some kids stay healthy," he replied, "and then we're going to have a party at my house."

I didn't know what he meant by helping kids stay healthy, but I knew I couldn't go. I had already promised my parents that I would carry out our family tradition.

My parents didn't care much for Halloween. Traditional trick-or-treating was out. My father was not about to let his children roam around the neighborhood begging for anything, especially candy. When I was young, we children had felt left out of the fun of the season. That was why my parents came up with a plan on how we could celebrate the holiday in a way they felt was appropriate.

My mother made lots of homemade divinity candy and tons of cookies. Then we dressed in costumes, and my mother drove us around the community, stopping only at the homes of the elderly. Instead of begging for treats, we took them some.

Many of them were widows and were lonely. They would invite us in and share stories, and it seemed to make life better for everyone.

When I became old enough to drive, I was the one who drove my younger brother and sister and me. But this year my younger siblings had parties to go to, and it was left to me, alone, to carry on the family tradition. I had already promised my mother that I would.

"I'm sorry," I told Lenny, "but I already have plans."

"You aren't going around visiting old people again, are you?" he asked. When I nodded, he laughed. "You're seventeen years old. That kind of stuff is for kids." When I said I still planned to do it, he just shook his head. "It's your loss. You're going to miss out on all of the fun. Maybe if you hurry you can catch the end of the party."

He laughed again, and, along with all of the other guys with him, teased me a bit more before heading off to catch the bus home.

All day Saturday, as I worked, I thought about it. I had never been to a Halloween party, and I kept telling myself that it would be okay if I skipped visiting the elderly this once. But then I would remember how much some of the widows looked forward to my visit, and I knew it did matter. I considered that maybe if I hurried I could still have time at the party, too.

That evening, my mother prepared a box for me with lots of plates full of candy and cookies covered with plastic wrap. On a piece of paper she listed out each house I was to visit.

As I stopped at each home, I was always invited in. Often I was offered hot chocolate, and the visits would go on longer than I planned.

I saved the home of Mrs. Levin for last. She was a sweet little widow whose children lived far away. She was very lonely and loved having company. My hope of catching some of the party faded as she told me about each of her children and then started sharing stories about when she and her husband were young. I realized I wouldn't be missed at the party, but my visit made a big difference to Mrs. Levin.

It was really late when I left Mrs. Levin's home, and I figured the party was probably over, so I just headed home. Even though I felt disappointment at missing the party, I had enjoyed my evening.

Lenny wasn't at church the next day, so I found his mother. "Where's Lenny?" I asked, laughing. "Is he still in bed from staying up too late partying?"

But there was no humor showing in her face as she answered. "He and the others with him were arrested for mugging little kids for their Halloween candy. They're still in jail."

Suddenly I knew what me meant by helping some kids stay healthy, and I was glad that that was one party I had missed.

Experience Is the Edge

Lenny came rushing into my first hour class waving a newspaper. "Howard, have you seen the newspaper?"

"Why, are you in the funny pages?" I asked.

He rolled his eyes. "Ha, ha. Very funny. I have a mind not to show you, now."

"Yeah," I replied. "Except for the fact that I could read it on my own, and then you would miss out on being the first to show me."

He knew I had him there. He shoved the newspaper at me. "Here. Look for yourself."

He had the paper open to the listings for the all-conference and all-state football team nominations. I smiled. "You made all-conference. Congratulations."

He shook his head. "No. I didn't. You did. And you made the all-state team, too."

I was surprised and scanned the list to see if he was telling the truth. Sure enough, I was listed in all-conference for offensive guard and on the state team for defensive tackle.

I guess the look on my face must have spoken my feelings because he laughed. "Hey, don't be so surprised. You're one of the best."

I scanned for one other name, and sure enough, Wade was there for all-conference offensive tackle.

I thought back to the previous year. I had been a junior. My dad had previously only allowed us to only compete in one sport because of the amount of work to be done on our farm. But when I kept up my chores and wrestling, too, he gave me permission to do more if I also kept good grades.

I could remember my first football practice. I had never even seen a game on television, so I made a ton of mistakes, and my teammates teased me a lot. That just steeled my resolve and made me work that much harder. I made the varsity cut, and everyone was surprised, but no one more than me. Coach just laughed when I asked him about it. "Howard, you've got more heart and determination than anyone I know."

Then came a day I will never forget. Coach pulled forty of us juniors who were on varsity into a special meeting. "Men," he said, "you have earned your varsity letter, but with the large, experienced senior squad we have, you will likely never get to play. I want to give you the opportunity to drop down to junior varsity if you would like. I can pretty much guarantee that if you do, you will get lots of playing time. Just come see me if you want to do that."

Everyone knew that would be a loss of prestige. The attention from the cheerleaders and other students would be gone. So when I told Lenny I was going to JV, he was surprised.

"You're crazy. No one cares about you on JV."

I laughed. "That might be a good thing, with as many mistakes as I make. But more important to me is the fact I joined up to play football, not to warm the bench."

Only two of the forty players went to JV — Wade and me. When the varsity players were honored in assemblies, we might be mentioned, but we were usually left out. When varsity lockers were decorated, ours were conspicuously left undone.

But on JV, Wade and I became a powerful duo as offensive tackle and offensive guard. I also found I had talent at defensive tackle, earning the honors of most tackles and most sacks for the season. I made lots of mistakes, but I learned a lot.

Then, in our senior year, Wade's and my experience showed as we moved to varsity and started in offense. I also started in defense and became the team kicker. We received lots of accolades, but mostly we had fun.

As my thoughts turned back to the paper, I scanned it for the names of the other thirty-eight who didn't go to JV, but none were there. Later, when Coach came to congratulate me, I mentioned that I was surprised none of them made it. "Many of them are more talented than I am," I said.

"That might be," he replied, "but experience and hard work will eventually edge out talent every time."

The Death of Private Orange

It was nearly November, and, as our high school English class was ending for the day, our teacher announced the next writing assignment. "For Veterans Day, each of you will write an interview paper. That means you are to interview someone and write about what you learned. The person you interview must be a veteran, and you are to ask them about what it was like to be in the armed services."

Most of the students groaned. Lenny was particularly vocal. "You mean we have to write something that some old person tells us?"

"I think you might find it more interesting than you think," the teacher said.

As we headed out the door, Lenny turned to me. "Howard, who are you going to interview?"

"I plan to interview my father," I replied. "How about you?"

"Probably my grandfather," he said. "But the big problem is once he gets started talking about the war, he never quits."

Later, when I asked my dad about what it was like in the army, he laughed. "How does a man explain the army? They try to kill you to make you strong, and they do stupid things just to teach you discipline."

"Like what?" I asked.

He thought for a moment and then answered, "Let me tell you a story.

"Basic training was hard. We marched and marched and drilled and marched some more. When it was finally over, we were told that we would be allowed a weekend furlough as soon as we could pass inspection.

"The first inspection didn't go well. Our sergeant found something wrong with every soldier. We did another week of marching and drill. Finally, the next weekend came. This time we worked much harder, and still, the sergeant found a few men who had something that wasn't quite right. Once more, we spent the week marching."

When the third weekend came, my dad said everyone was determined to have everything perfect. They shined shoes, spruced up uniforms, and worked to get everything to perfection. The sergeant moved from man to man, finding nothing out of line.

When he reached the last man, the sergeant made him open his duffle bag. When he did, out rolled an orange.

"Is food allowed in your duffle bag, Private?" the sergeant demanded.

"No, Sir," the soldier replied.

"And let me tell you why," the sergeant said, getting right up nose to nose with the man. "The reason is because it would suffocate in there with your socks. I, therefore, declare Private Orange to have died in your duffle bag." He then turned to the full group of men. "Doesn't Private Orange deserve a proper burial?"

"Yes, Sir," the men all answered unenthusiastically.

"As soon as he has received his proper burial," the sergeant said, "you can all go on furlough."

The sergeant chose the place for the grave, a horrible, hard packed piece of land. The men took turns chiseling through the soil. After a six foot deep grave was dug, Private Orange was buried with military honors.

As soon as the service was over, the men quickly filled in the grave and then assembled, excited to go on furlough.

"Well done, men," the sergeant said. "But did you make sure to bury him face up?"

"What's face up, Sir?" one soldier asked.

"He does have a navel," the sergeant replied. "And a person's navel is on the same side as his face."

The men dug up the orange, made sure it was oriented

properly, and buried it again. By the time they finally finished, they had only time for a very short furlough.

When my dad finished his story, he smiled. "Military intelligence is an oxymoron, but they do teach you discipline."

Gratitude for What We Have

It had been a hard year for our family. My father had formed a partnership with a man he had trusted, but the man ended up taking advantage of my father's trust and honesty. The man took all of the incoming money, but left my father with the bills. The partnership was broken, leaving my father with no income and hard-pressed to pay the money owed. But he was determined to do so in order to preserve his good name.

Although there was little money for things like school clothes, we always had enough to eat. We raised a big garden, and it and our farm produced plenty of food. There were times when we children felt the sting of teasing from others because our clothes, though clean and neat, were not the newest style. There were times when we felt left out because other kids our age could go to the evening show at the theater and we couldn't. But when a new family, the Tawsons, moved in near us, we soon realized how lucky we were.

We saw them unloading the moving van and went to help. The children's clothes were even more worn than ours, but the main thing that we noticed was how thin they were. The mother was thin as well, but the father was dressed nicely and was the opposite of thin. The contrast was so stark it was hard not to notice.

As our family helped them move their belongings into the house, we learned little about them. The mother had a job teaching in a local school, while the husband was unemployed. The children said nothing. When my mother brought over a house warming dinner to finish off our welcome, the Tawson children eyed the food hungrily. When it was set on the table, they ate as if they had fasted for days.

When our family returned home, my father spoke what was on everyone's mind. "Something is not right there."

It was only a short time later when we learned more. My father had gone to the hardware store to get some hinges to fix a broken door on our barn. While passing the local bar, he saw Mr. Tawson inside drinking and gambling. My father didn't think too much of it, but that same day, my mother caught some of the Tawson children stealing food from our pantry.

"What are you doing?" she demanded.

The children hung their heads but said nothing. My mother took them home and visited with their mother. Mrs. Tawson was embarrassed.

"I'm sorry," she said. "But we have nothing in the house to eat."

"Doesn't your job provide enough?" my mother asked.

Mrs. Tawson could not look my mother in the eye and seemed reluctant to talk, but the situation had torn the mask from the silence. "My husband takes my paychecks and gives me very little back to buy food with. The children are always hungry."

"What does he do with the money?" my mother asked.

"He said that was none of my business," Mrs. Tawson answered tearfully. "Unfortunately, sometimes he uses what food he allows us to have as incentive to make sure we do as he demands." She looked pleadingly at my mother. "Please don't tell him I said anything."

"You tell your children they don't need to steal," my mother said. "They can have food, though I may expect some help weeding the garden or doing other chores in exchange."

That evening, as my mother told my father what had happened, they started piecing it all together.

From then on, the Tawson children were often helping with chores, and, in return, they would eat with us and take food home.

And as we grew to understand their situation, our desires for what we didn't have changed to gratitude for how good our lives really were.

My parents found out that Mr. Tawson not only refused to hold a job, but took most of his wife's paycheck for himself, leaving almost nothing for her to purchase food to feed herself and their children. There were few things in life that disgusted my father more than a man who would not take care of his family.

Although our family had had some financial setbacks and had very little in the way of money, we had plenty of food from our farm. My parents started providing the Tawson children with food, and, in return, they helped us with our chores.

But Thanksgiving was coming, and the thought of Mrs. Tawson and her family not having a Thanksgiving feast bothered my father. We didn't grow turkeys on our farm, and we couldn't afford to purchase one. But my father was a good hunter, so the day before Thanksgiving he had a talk with my mother.

"I am going down to the river and shoot a goose," my father said. "I plan to stop on the way home and invite the Tawsons over for Thanksgiving dinner. We may not have turkey, but we will have plenty."

"Won't it bother you having Mr. Tawson over?" my mother asked. "I know how he disgusts you."

My father shrugged. "It's Thanksgiving, and he needs to eat, too."

My father left with his gun, and a couple hours later he returned with one of the biggest geese we had ever seen. He gave it to my mother to clean and prepare.

"How did it go at the Tawson's home?" my mother asked.

He smiled. "Mr. Tawson scowled, but the rest of the family were so excited to have a place to go for dinner that they could hardly contain themselves."

There was always lots of farm work to do, and the Tawson

boys came over that afternoon to help. They ate with us and, as usual, took food home as pay. The whole time, the only thing they could talk about was coming for Thanksgiving dinner.

The next day, as was usual for Thanksgiving, we worked until noon. From that point on the day was ours to enjoy. About then the Tawson family showed up. At least, they all did except for Mr. Tawson. He chose to head in to the local bar.

Our home, by that time, smelled better than the finest restaurant. The smell of the roasting goose permeated the air, interspersed with the sweet aroma of apple, gooseberry, pumpkin, and mincemeat pies. On the counter, my mother had tray after tray of homemade rolls ready to go into the oven when the goose came out.

Mrs. Tawson rolled up her sleeves and started helping my mother. The aroma kept enticing the children from both families into the kitchen, but those who weren't old enough to help were always shooed away.

When the goose came out and the rolls were put in, the smell was almost irresistible. My mother made gravy from the drippings of the meat, and by the time the first rolls were done, dinner was ready.

We sat at the table and offered a prayer of thanks, and as everyone started to eat, the noisy chatter died down. The youngest Tawson was a three-year-old girl named Melanie. She was a wisp of a child. She sat on a pile of books on a chair, bringing her chin just above the table. From that level she scooped the food off of her plate right into her mouth. My father's eyes sparkled as he watched her. She ate multiple platefuls until she couldn't hold another bite. When she finished, she smiled happily.

When Mrs. Tawson thanked my parents for the meal, my father smiled as he replied, "Thanksgiving always tastes better when it's shared."

Mutton Chops

All of this fall people have asked me why I looked like I do, so let me explain.

My two youngest daughters wanted to try out for the local production of *A Christmas Carol*, so I joined them for some father-daughter time. We filled out the audition papers, and one question asked what part we would consider playing. I put that I would be happy with no part at all and could just work on my next book while I waited for my daughters. But, I wrote, if they had a small part that needed to be filled, I would help out.

They asked me to read the part for Scrooge, and I did. Later that evening they called and asked me to come for callbacks. I did, and the next day I received an email asking me to take that part.

I had to consider it for a while. I had just had knee replacement surgery, and besides spending lots of time in therapy, I was still in a lot of pain. In addition, I had extra work at the university and was also trying to prepare my next book for publication. As I took the few days allotted for me to respond, one of the people in charge said they hoped I would take the part because Scrooge needed to be mean, and I was the only one who acted mean enough. I wasn't sure if that was a compliment or not, but I did decide to take the part.

Once I had accepted, I was asked if I could grow mutton chops for it. For those who don't know, chops are long sideburns to the chin. Because I work at a religious university with a dress and grooming code in which chops are not allowed, it took a little time to get permission. But within two weeks, the chops had come in thick, I felt that I already looked really stupid, and I still had months to go.

I teach music to the children at the church I attend, and they hadn't seen me for those two weeks, so they were curious as to why

I looked like I did. "Well," I joked, "I am in a play, and back in that time period, men would compete to see how ugly they could get."

One darling little four-year-old excitedly worked to get my attention. When I called on her, she spoke enthusiastically. "You are doing a good job. I think you're going to win."

My students at the college started calling me Wolverine, and I didn't even know what that meant until one of them brought me a picture from X-Men.

One Sunday afternoon I lay down for a nap. In the middle of it, a fly landed on my newly grown whiskers. In my sleep I reached up to swat it away. In doing so my hand brushed my new facial hair, and, in my sleepy state, I thought some kind of caterpillar was crawling on my face. I grabbed it and pulled, and the pain brought me completely out of my sleep.

When my daughter and her children came to visit from California, my three-year-old grandson looked at me and said, "Grandpa, you look . . . " He paused, so I filled in.

"Stupid?"

He nodded. "Yeah."

When my twenty-two-year-old son came home from college for Thanksgiving, he looked at me and just started laughing, unable to talk. People that I know and say hi to just stare at me. Others, knowing where I work, ask if I have retired. Seriously, I'm not that old.

And today, I went to pick up my daughter. She was at an after-school activity. I parked the van and went in to tell her I was ready to go home. I finally found a group in the cafeteria that looked like it might be hers. As I approached them, one girl in the group turned and stared at me. She then turned back to the others and whispered, "Don't look now, but there is a really creepy guy here." My daughter poked her head up above the group, saw me, and called out, "Hi, Dad."

But I'm a grown man, so why would looking like this bother

me? I mean, I only have thirteen days, five hours, and twenty minutes until the end of the last performance when I can shave my chops off, but who's counting?

One Ugly Bike

Martin, my colleague, said, "Your bike is so ugly, I want you to ride at least 100 yards away from me so no one knows I know you."

"It's not that ugly," I said.

"It is that ugly," he replied.

We were twenty years old, living and working in New York, and bikes were our only means of transportation. After my previous one was stolen, I bought a girl's ugly three-speed that was stuck in third gear. It only cost six dollars, it was never stolen even when I didn't lock it up, and, most important to me, it always worked.

Sometimes trying to get it moving with it in third gear was a challenge. If I started from a full stop, I could hardly press the pedals. But I found out that if I ran alongside of it and then jumped on, I had enough momentum to get it moving more easily.

This embarrassed Martin even more, and I found that he did try to ride a good distance ahead of me. When we ended up being stopped at the same stoplight, intersection, or the like, when we started out again he would try to take off quickly so he could put some distance between us. He continued to tell me how ugly my bike was, and I continued to tell him it wasn't that bad.

The first Sunday I rode it to church, I left it leaning against the fence, as usual. One of the members of the congregation came into the meeting we were attending. "I think I have just seen the ugliest bike in the world," he said, "and it has been abandoned by the church fence."

Without disclosing that it was mine, I asked, "Why do you think it was abandoned?"

"Well," he replied, "I'm sure no one in their right mind would ride something that ugly, and we are a church, so someone probably left it as a donation to charity."

"That's not a donation," Martin told the man. "That's Howard's bike."

Later that week, Martin and I had a meeting with other young men and young women our age. We arrived early, and Martin suggested that I park my bike behind the building so no one would see it. I reluctantly agreed and took it out back. I leaned it against the fence near where the dumpster was sitting.

Just before our meeting started, one of the other young men came in. "You wouldn't believe what I saw out back," he said. "It has to be the world's ugliest bike. Someone put it by the dumpster. Apparently they wanted to throw it away but couldn't get it up into it, so I did."

My heart started to pound. As I ran to save my bike, I heard Martin laughing as he called after me, "Howard, it is that ugly!"

I climbed into the dumpster and lifted my bike out. By the time I climbed back out myself, my clothes were less than sanitary. I dropped to the ground, turned around, and there was the whole group. Martin had led them out to see my bike.

"Howard, don't tell me you ride that bike," the guy that threw it away said.

"It's not that ugly," I replied.

Martin nodded. "It is that ugly."

Later that week, Martin and I were out working. A little child who was about eight years old came up to me. "Hey, Misser, did you buy dat bike or steal it?" he asked.

"I bought it," I replied.

"How much did you pay for it?"

"I paid six bucks," I told him.

He shook his head. "Man, you need to go home and let yo' mamma slap you. You got ripped off."

Martin grinned and said, "It *is* that ugly."

Shop with a Cop

My son Scott has always wanted to serve his community and his country, but he didn't see the military as an option for himself. So when he learned that the local sheriff's department was looking for some reserve deputies to help when needed, he decided that might be his opportunity. After weeks of intensive training, the day of graduation finally came. It wasn't long before he was going on patrols with the regular deputies and helping where he could.

But then came an assignment he hadn't considered before. Through the year the community raised money for "Shop with a Cop" to allow police officers to take underprivileged children Christmas shopping. A local fast-food restaurant also donates a meal for the shoppers.

Usually there are far more children in need than funds to go around, but this particular year there were extra fund-raisers, and enough money was collected to help all of the children listed. But this meant that there were not enough regular officers to fill the need, so the reserve deputies were asked to help out.

Scott gladly accepted the opportunity to spend time with one of the children and was assigned to take an eight-year-old boy named David. When Scott took David out to eat, David, accustomed to having very little money, only ordered a small hamburger and a water. Scott, knowing that wasn't sufficient, more than quadrupled the order for him. David was amazed at the amount of food but happily ate it.

When it came time to go shopping, Scott took David to a local department store. He was sure David would want some toys for himself, so that was where they started. But David was not interested in that.

"Would you like to look at something else?" Scott asked.

David nodded. "Can we look at clothes? I would like to get a new coat."

That was when Scott noticed how threadbare the coat was that David was wearing, and he thought that he should have realized David would want a new one. But when Scott took him over to the boys' clothing section of the store and showed him the coats, David was still not interested. Instead, he walked over to the girls' section. Suddenly his eyes lit up. He pulled a beautiful coat from the girls' rack.

"Do you think this would fit a six-year-old girl?" David asked.

"Who is six years old?" Scott asked.

"My sister," David replied. "She really needs a new coat."

Scott instantly gained a deeper appreciation for this little boy and his situation. But he wasn't sure what size a six-year-old girl would wear, so he called our home to talk to his mother. She helped them figure out the right size, and soon they had the perfect coat. There was still money left, so Scott suggested that David buy a coat for himself. Instead, he wanted to use what was left to buy coats for his mother and his father. When that was done, the money was gone and David was happy.

But Scott was not. He had watched this little boy selflessly thinking of his family and never thinking of himself. David's worn and tattered coat was far too small for him and too light to hold out the extreme Idaho cold.

Before they turned to go, Scott said, "David, there is one more thing we need to buy."

"Is there more money?" David asked.

Scott shook his head. "No, but this is my present."

Scott took David to the coat rack for boys and chose the warmest coat he could find. They tried a couple before they found the perfect one. Although Scott was a college student and on a tight budget, he found that the smile on David's face was generous pay.

That year, although Scott thought he was doing a good service in helping a little child, he instead became the beneficiary as an eight-year-old boy taught him what Christmas was all about.

Acting on Good Intentions

My dad used to say that good intentions are never enough; they must be acted upon. Still, I find myself too often with good intentions on which I don't follow through. That was what was happening that holiday season. I was busy with preparation for Thanksgiving when I had a feeling that I should go visit my friend Stan, who was in a nursing home.

I couldn't find time in my schedule, so I decided I would visit him right after Thanksgiving. But Thanksgiving came and went, and it seemed like instead of having more time, I had less. As Christmas approached, I still hadn't visited Stan.

Then, one Sunday, I felt a very strong feeling that I needed to visit him that very day. The feeling grew stronger as the day progressed. By evening time I could not get it to go away. My wife, Donna, was having a choir practice, and I was the only bass who was going to be there. But not long before practice was to start, I could ignore the feeling no longer and told her I needed to visit Stan before he went to bed.

"But what about choir?" she asked.

"Start without me," I replied, "and I will do my best to get back for part of it."

My youngest daughter said she wanted to go with me, so together we made the twenty-minute drive to the nursing home. Once there, we made our way to Stan's room and looked through the open door.

Stan was sitting on the edge of his bed with the television blaring. But he had his back to it and was paying it no attention. Instead, he was sitting motionless, dressed in his pajamas, his head bowed.

"Hey, Stan," I called from the doorway. "How are you doing?"

He looked up, and I could see that he had tears rolling down his cheeks. He stared at us for a moment, and after he realized who we were, a smile spread across his face and seemed to engulf him.

"I thought my friends had forgotten that it was my birthday," he said. "I had been praying all day that someone would remember and come, but no one did, so I decided I would just get ready for bed."

I knew his family would have remembered, but he had apparently hoped his friends would, too. He struggled to his feet. He was a tough old farmer, not one to show emotion, but when we walked over, he threw his arms around me. "Thanks for remembering," he said.

I didn't tell him I hadn't even known it was his birthday, but I did feel strange as I thought about the feeling I had felt all day.

Stan sat back down on his bed, and my daughter and I pulled up chairs. We visited for a long time. He told us stories about his service in World War II, priceless stories from a generation that was quickly fading away. I had heard most of them over the years, but my daughter hadn't, and she was enthralled by them. He talked about meeting and marrying his wonderful wife, who had passed on not very long before he came to this place. He talked about his years of farming and raising his children. He proudly told us what each of them was doing.

I knew that choir practice had already been running for quite some time, but I felt a need to stay with Stan, and I knew my good wife would understand. Stan talked until he grew tired, and the attendant came to help him get ready for bed. He asked us to stay until he was tucked in for the night, and we did. As we prepared to leave, he took one of our hands in each of his and thanked us for coming. He then lay back on his pillow and drowsed off with a smile on his face as we tiptoed from the room.

As we drove home, thinking of the events of the day, I made a commitment for the new year to try more often not to let my good intentions go by without acting on them.

A Personal Foul for a Band

David waited quite a while for his friend John to show up because they were supposed to have a band trombone sectional. David was the section leader, and he needed John. The two of them were the only seniors in their section, and John's talent was necessary to help the younger band members. David called John's cell phone, but there was no answer. After some time, David was finally forced to run the practice without him.

It was a short practice, after which he looked up John's home number and called it. He was not there, and his family said he had been at the school the whole time, so David went looking for him. His search finally led him to the gym, where a company was installing a new scoreboard system. There he found John sitting in the bleachers, very alert, holding his trombone in hand. No one else besides John and the scoreboard company technicians were in the gym, so David's curiosity forced him to stop and watch his friend.

When the company would tested something on the new scoreboard and sounded the buzzer, John would immediately blow into his trombone. After watching this for a short time, David walked over to the bleachers where John was seated.

"John," David said, "did you know you missed sectional?"

"I did?" John replied. He paused as the realization settled on him. "Oh, we did have that today, didn't we? I'm sorry. But I heard them blowing this buzzer. It sounded almost like our trombone section, and I've been trying to duplicate it."

At that instant the buzzer sounded again, and John tried to imitate it, but there was something slightly different. David realized it didn't sound like one trombone, but it did sound like their section. He ran to retrieve his instrument and then hurried back.

"Let's try it together," he said.

The next time the buzzer sounded, John played and David

added a slight overtone. The sound was so close to the buzzer that the men working on the scoreboard checked to see why their buzzer had gone off of its own accord. David and John knew it wasn't perfect, but they knew they could make it so, and they laughed and high-fived each other.

They worked on perfecting it but dared not use it at a home game when their own score keepers would be blamed. However, the buzzers sound just about the same at every school, so the first time they played in the pep band at an away game against their strongest rival, they were ready. The first time a member of the opposing team shot from the foul line, they played. The sound they made scared the shooter, and the ball went wide of its mark.

Their sound may not have been perfect, but it fooled almost everyone. The ref was perturbed and yelled at the score keepers. The score keepers looked at their equipment, stunned that it would sound off on its own.

David and John continued their mischief. Even though the reverberation of the hall made it impossible for anyone to distinguish where the sound came from, it soon became obvious to all that it only occurred when the home team was about to make a shot. That, of course, meant that it had to be the visiting team's side. Still, it was nearly halftime before the refs were sure it was the band, and by then the home team was so unnerved by it that they had a huge deficit.

To that point it had already been an unprecedented game, and once the refs were sure who the culprit was, they did something else unprecedented: they called the first personal foul on a band that anyone could ever remember.

But this raises a final question: If a band receives five personal fouls, can they be ejected from the game?

A Funeral and a Memory

(All of my stories are based on a true event, but I don't always follow exact facts, and they, therefore, would be considered fiction. However, this story and the next two are as factual as I could make them.)

I went to a funeral this week for my former high school teacher, Sam Christiansen. It brought back lots of memories, some different from what you might expect. The main one was not even from school. It was from the summer before my junior year.

That summer had been hot, and the work was never-ending. One day my father sent me to get some parts from the hardware store. There I ran into my good friend and cousin, Lane.

"Hey, what worthless things are you doing with yourself this summer?" he asked.

I laughed. "Well, right now we are finishing up some hay hauling. How about you?"

He smiled his big smile. "Well, Mr. Bagoo, I am here to get some camping things. Our scout troop is heading to Shoshone Lake." Then he laughed again. "Think of me while you're hard at work, because I won't be thinking about you while I'm fishing."

I, too, laughed as we headed our separate ways. Lane and I were distant cousins but close friends. He and I worked side by side in football and were formidable together. In addition, he was my wrestling partner. His happy, nonchalant attitude was a good balance to my serious one.

I went back to work and thought nothing of our meeting until a couple of days later. An unexpected storm had come through the area the previous day, and we were concerned about the possibility of more storms coming, so we were desperately trying to get the last of the hay in. I had brought in the final truckload and was busily unloading it, with the heat of the day beating the sweat out of me, when my mother came rushing out.

"Daris, something has happened. You better come into the

house."

I jumped down from the haystack and followed her. It took a while for the full news to be known, but what we heard was disconcerting.

Lane and the others of his troop, all friends of mine, had been crossing Shoshone Lake in the heart of Yellowstone. The lead canoes were nearing the north shore of the lake, perhaps only thirty yards away from it, when, in an instant, a powerful storm came up, blowing against them and causing huge whitecap waves.

Some of them were thrown into the lake, but in one small canoe, Kim Bischoff and Brant Kerbs fought hard to reach the shore. After exhausting their strength, unable to fight any longer, they turned around and went quickly with the wind the many miles back across the lake. When they landed, to everyone's surprise, they found themselves in the campsite of two of our high school teachers, Sam Christiansen and Darrel Gibbons.

These two teachers, finding out others on the lake were in trouble, decided they had to attempt a rescue. Taking the advice of Darrel's father, who was at the camp with them, they lashed oars across their two canoes to give them the added stability of a double-hulled craft. They fought their way out into the lake three times to pick up the six that were known to have been thrown into the icy water.

As darkness settled in, eight of the group were safely at the camp, but there was no sign or word of the last two, Lane and Van. Since they had been in the lead and almost to the north shore, all hoped that they had made it safely. When my mother called me in that day, the only word we had of them was that they were still missing, and I prayed desperately that my friends would be found safe. But it wasn't to be. The next day I learned that they hadn't made it.

As I sat at the funeral this week for our teacher, Sam Christiansen, I thought of that summer day when I attended Lane and

Van's funeral. It was a peaceful July morning, a contrast to the turbulence that had come into our lives. I sat there as one of the many pallbearers, all friends of the two young men. I knew I would not again hear Lane call me Mr. Bagoo, and in my sixteen-year-old heart I wondered why life was the way it was.

But as time went by, my questions turned to gratitude that our two teachers had miraculously been there and were brave enough and had enough love and skill to save as many lives as they did.

Tragedy and Unity

That fall, as we prepared for our first high school football game of the season, our team was very much as it had always been. Though we worked and practiced together, we were not unified.

I could not remember it ever being any different. If something wasn't going just right, the backs blamed the linemen, the linemen blamed the backs, and the problems compounded with plenty of blame to go around.

But something else had happened that summer that had penetrated deep into our hearts. Due to a freak storm, we had lost two of our close friends, Lane and Van, in a canoeing accident on Shoshone Lake in Yellowstone National Park.

Coach Sam came one day to watch us practice. He taught government, economics, and U.S. history. He no longer coached, but he could see our disunity. He had a great love for us, his students, and it bothered him. Perhaps he was bothered more by it than he normally would have been because he was at a camp on Shoshone Lake the day of the accident. He was one of the men who had seen the trouble the scout troop had been in and had gone to their rescue, saving those they could find. And the next morning, he was one of the first to see the articles from Lane and Van's canoe washed up on shore, realizing they hadn't made it.

Coach Sam came to our first game. With our team's disharmony, we should have lost, but we received some lucky breaks and eked out a win. The win only added to the problems, as many acted as if they alone had made it possible.

Coach Sam couldn't stand it anymore. He came to our team meeting before practice and asked the coaches for permission to speak to us. He told us what he had seen in our attitudes toward each other and how much it bothered him.

"I don't care if you win another game this whole year," he

said. "But if you treat each other the way you are, instead of as the friends and teammates you should be, I don't think I can bear to watch another game."

He then reached inside a little bag and pulled out a small tin drinking cup. His eyes filled with tears, and his voice choked as he held it up. "This last summer, a tragedy struck our small school and cut deeply into our community. Many of you were good friends with Lane and Van and felt that loss. The next morning after that fateful day, as I walked along the water's edge, hoping to see a campfire in the distance indicating they were safe, I instead found this cup washed ashore from their sunken canoe. That was when I knew they hadn't made it."

As he continued, he passed it around for each of us to look at and to hold. "I have kept it as a reminder of how fragile life is and how important friendships are. I now give it to you, as a team, to remind you of the same thing."

As my turn came to hold the cup, I took it and turned it over. It was nothing beautiful or spectacular to look at, only simple, weathered tin, but the memory it brought burned deep in my soul. Lane and I were distant cousins and close friends. He had been my wrestling partner. I was a lineman and he was a back. When he had a choice, he chose to run my side of the line. I had opened many holes for him. He had always trusted me to do my part.

As I struggled to hold back the tears that my feelings were creating, Coach Sam finished. "Let this be your victory cup. Whether it takes you to a district and a state championship is not important. But if it takes you to the victory of eternal friendship and unity, then it will have done its job, and perhaps Lane and Van will not have died in vain."

And that season, that was exactly what our victory cup did for us.

A Motivational Teacher

I stopped after class to talk with my teacher, Coach Sam. I was going to the state wrestling tournament and would be missing a big quiz in my U.S. history class. I asked him if I could make it up when I returned or if he wanted me to take it before I left.

"I'll tell you what," he said. "If you win, I'll let you make it up when you get back."

I was a junior and had worked really hard in wrestling. I had won the district championship but was looking at some tough competition at state. I knew there were some seniors in my weight from other schools that had big reputations.

"What if I lose?" I asked.

"Just don't plan on losing," he replied, "and you won't have to cross that bridge."

I went to state and fought some of the toughest matches of my life. I progressed quite well but was injured in my third match. And even though I continued to wrestle, the pain in my knee reduced my ability to compete effectively. But I must admit that, in many ways, I beat myself as I worried unnecessarily about the other wrestlers' reputations and experience. I did not come home with the state title.

When I came back to class on Monday and asked Coach Sam about taking the quiz, he said, "I understand you didn't win state." I verified that was true. "Well, then," he continued, "I'm afraid it is going to have to count as a missed quiz and a zero. But since I drop the lowest one for the semester, it shouldn't hurt you."

"But I studied hard for it, and I know I can do well," I complained. "Besides, I was gone for a school excused activity."

"Howard," he said, "what do you think a teacher's job is?"

"To teach," I replied.

"That is only part of it. A teacher is to encourage, to

motivate, and to help students reach their full potential and believe in themselves. I believe you had the ability to win state, but apparently I believed in you more than you did. To me, your excused absence is only valid if you made full use of your time and ability, and I don't believe you did that."

No amount of disagreement on my part could dissuade him from his decision. He was determined that I could have won.

The next year I again won district, and as if history was repeating itself, I had a big U.S. government quiz on the weekend of the state tournament. I again approached Coach Sam about taking it when I got back.

"If you don't win, well, you know the answer, don't you?" he replied.

I had trained hard through the year, and though I was more experienced and was considered by many to be one of the best wrestlers in the state, I had also struggled with a tough case of pneumonia that had weakened my lungs. I had my doubts, but Coach Sam expressed his belief in me.

I went to state, and the farther I moved through the tournament, the more tired my lungs became, and, in turn, the less energy I had. Going into the championship match, I thought of my desire for the state title and the desire to live up to Coach Sam's belief in me. I somehow found energy I didn't even know I had. I won, though I nearly passed out afterward from the exertion.

I was too sick to return to school the next Monday, but when I walked into U.S. government the first hour on Tuesday morning, Coach Sam had the class give me a standing ovation.

"Does that mean I get an automatic 100% on the missed quiz since I got an automatic 0 last year?" I asked.

"No," Coach Sam said, "but you do get to take it."

I did well on the quiz, but most important, because of good teachers, I feel I have done well in life. Thanks, Coach Sam, for believing in me.

I don't know if anyone ever sees anything fun in want-ad postings, but sometimes the personality of the person doing the posting really shows through. Between that and the fact that sometimes the post probably doesn't come out quite like the person intended, the humor in them can brighten my day. I like to collect the ones that make me smile, and I thought I'd share some of them with you.

On Craig's List: Wedding table cameras. Purchased off tietheknot.com for $4.99 each, then husband forgot to bring them on our wedding day!!!! (It's still a touchy subject!) Still in the plastic, contains 400-speed film and a small tent-style instruction card. I would like these gone so I can get on with my marriage and not have to see them unused anymore.

On Craig's List: Cow named Bessy. Would like to trade for cow of no name. Is full grown. Was grain fed and raised for meat, but made the mistake of naming her at the time we fed her as a calf from a bottle. If you have a similar cow to trade, will trade straight across.

On Freecycle: Our puppy died, giving away the bones.

On Freecycle: Free, talking doll. Freaks me out seriously. I can't take it in my house anymore, and I can fully blame my father and the science fiction channel. It plays peekaboo and my toddler loves it, but I can't keep it, seriously. I keep expecting it to look at me and say, "I'm talking, Jane." Please e-mail for address.

On Freecycle: Free hen. Her companion hen is gone and she is depressed. She needs to be with other hens! I will not give her to someone who doesn't already have some! She is super sweet and amazingly tame because we raised her from like a week old. She is laying even in winter because we have had a heat lamp on her (but the heat lamp we are not giving away). You will need your own cage, however. We are keeping ours. I repeat, you cannot have our cage. (I say this because people have stolen things I said were not up for grabs before.) We have a large feeder and a large waterer and a huge barely broken into bag of scratch for her, (but she likes the other feed better). Please call me to set up a time and get our address. Thanks. I am emotionally attached, so do not respond if you are wanting to kill her!!! I want her to go to a good home, maybe with kids who can love her, and I don't mean in a stew.

A second posting on FreeCycle: To the Lady who got my Hen: Her long-lost friend finally returned home. If you would like her as well, please call me.

Craig's List: It's a long shot but I'm looking for the person who bought a pair of brown, felt sole wading boots from a thrift store in Idaho Falls. There were two pair of the same kind and I believe that you mismatched them and have two different sizes (as I do now). LOL Let me know and we can swap them out.

On Freecyle: Free, one night stand. Beautiful and in good shape. Well built with nice, smooth curves. Beautiful drawers. Not too old. Slim and light tan/blonde, though slightly greying from being in sunlight. Legs are beautiful, and top is, too. To reply, please call. . .

A second posting on FreeCycle: All right. For all of you clueless idiots. A night stand is a little piece of furniture that goes by your bed, and I happen to have one of them. And it is in good shape, and well built. If you aren't interested in furniture, don't call me!

Athletic Discipline

As I stepped into the college wrestling room for the first time, I was greeted by posters hung all around the walls that I assume were supposed to motivate us. Oh, there were the usual ones like, "No pain, no gain." But there were a few like "Second place is only another name for the first place loser," for which I questioned the motivational value.

When it was time to begin, Coach walked in holding a clipboard. "To start each practice," he said, "we will begin with the roll call sit."

The big heavyweight groaned. "Oh, man, I hate that part of practice."

"Did you say something, Williams?" Coach asked.

"I was just saying that I think I could live without it."

Coach then told Williams to demonstrate it. He sighed but walked to the wall and obediently sat against it as if he were sitting in an invisible chair. Coach then ordered us to do the same. We did so, and I soon realized why the older wrestlers hated it. My calves and hamstrings started begging for mercy. As we stayed in that position, Coach informed us that we would stay there each day until roll call was over. He then started. After he called each name, the wrestler would quickly answer "here" to move things along. But Coach was in no hurry and would take his time getting to the next name.

Once, he called a name for which no one answered. He acted like he was going to mark it down but then stopped. "Can you believe it? The lead in my pencil is broken."

He casually walked to the other end of the room to see if he could find another one, keeping an eye on us to make sure we didn't change positions. He rummaged through his stuff for what seemed like an hour before returning and finally marking the absence. By the time he did, everyone was in extreme pain, and there was some mumbling among the wrestlers about making the absent person have a punishment of his own the next day.

Coach eventually called the next name as if he didn't have a care in the world. By the time we finished the roll, and he told us to sit on the mat, my legs were locked into a permanent charley horse.

"As you can see," Coach said, "wrestling is all about discipline and teamwork. You may have thought wrestling was an individual sport, but it is far from it. The decisions you make, like deciding to skip practice, affect everyone."

"And I would suggest you don't even think about being late," Williams said.

"Good point, Williams," Coach said. "But is it me who metes out the punishment?"

"No, Sir," Williams replied.

"Who does?" Coach asked.

"The team does, Sir."

"As they do for pretty much everything," Coach added.

I wondered what the team punishment was, but I was definitely not anxious to find out. Unfortunately, a few days later I was to learn about it. I arrived at the dressing room on time but had forgotten my lock combination. By the time I was able to get it from the athletic office and get dressed, I was late. When I stepped into the wrestling room, roll call was over, and I could see by the look on everyone's face that they were not happy with my absence.

They all stood in a line and spread their legs. I had to crawl through the tunnel of legs, and they all got to whack my backside. When I got to Williams, he hit me so hard that I rolled end over end twice, all the way to the wall.

While those at the end of the line complained they didn't get to whack me, Williams just grinned. "I took care of it for all of you." He then turned to me. "Don't you just love that part of practice?"

I thought I personally could have lived without it.

Valentine's Day Problems

I was almost seventeen, and the Valentine's Day girls-choice dance was to be my first date. I had not yet been on a date, because when it came to dealings with those of the opposite gender, I was extremely timid.

There would be four of us together — my date, her friend, her friend's date, and me. I was the only one with access to a car, so I would be driving.

The problem was that the car I had access to was getting older and had some problems. The biggest problem was that the transmission was going out. When the car started out from a stopped position, the transmission would jump into second gear, and then drop back to first gear, then to second, then back to first, and so on, until it got up to about thirty miles per hour. At that point, it would finally stay in one gear and the driving would smooth out. This problem caused the car to lurch and buck like a bronc coming out of the gate at a rodeo.

I had informed the others in our group about this, and they said they were okay with it, especially since it was the only car available.

At school on Friday, the day before the big dance, my date came and checked once more to make sure I would have a car. When I told her I would, she smiled her beautiful smile. "It will be fun. We are going to have a wonderful dinner with sparkling grape juice and everything."

After she left, I turned to my friend, Lenny, who was with me. "What is sparkling grape juice?" I asked.

"It's like wine," he answered.

"Like wine?"

My naiveté must have shown in the concerned look on my face because he laughed. "Don't worry—it's not alcoholic. It just tastes like wine, bites like wine, and smells like wine."

"Okay," I said, still not sure.

We did have a lot of fun the night of the dance. The girls had spent the day preparing the food, and it was very good. The sparkling grape juice was delicious, and we all drank plenty, though all the bubbles in it made us feel a bit queasy. Finally, it was time to go to the dance.

I tried to ease the car out onto the road as carefully as I could, hoping it would go smoothly, but the car was quite rebellious and would have none of it. It bucked, jerked, and chugged. The sloshing, bubbly grape juice in our stomachs made them churn. My date's friend said, "I think I am going to barf."

Luckily, she didn't, and everyone soon felt better as the car smoothed out for the long ride into town. But there was one more place where we had to come to a complete stop. After we stopped there, I once more carefully started forward. But even more than before, the car bucked, jumped, and lurched. I felt sick, but the others were having an even harder time.

Just as the car was settling down, I saw red and blue lights flashing in my rear view mirror. I pulled over, and the police officer came up and shined his flashlight in my face. He then swung it around to look at the others in the car who were swallowing air to keep from losing their dinner. He swung the light back to me and spoke gruffly. "I saw how you drove away from that stop sign. Have you been drinking?"

"No, officer," I said.

He looked at me suspiciously and then said, "Well, I can see you are all dressed to go to the dance. I won't make you walk a line. Just let me smell your breath."

That was when I remembered Lenny's line about how sparkling grape juice smelled like wine. I quickly tried to explain about the car's transmission and the sparkling grape juice. When I finished, he was grinning. "All right," he said. "I think you can go."

"Thanks for understanding," I replied.

"Oh, I believe you," he said, laughing. "No one that was drunk could make up a story half that good. I can't wait to share this one with the other officers."

And with that, he let us go, and we headed on our way, with our car staggering its way to the dance.

February is scout month, and it always reminds me of the eighteen boys who were in my troop when I was scoutmaster. On one particular evening, we were just starting scouts when a new boy came in. He looked lost, so I went over to greet him. "May I help you?"

He nodded. "I was told that a scout troop met here on Tuesday nights, and I was hoping to join them."

"That would be us," I said, holding out my hand to shake his. "I'm the scoutmaster."

He cautiously took my hand. "But no one is wearing a uniform."

Just then, Gordy came over. "Hey, David, come to join us?"

David nodded. "This is scouts, right?"

"Of course," Gordy replied. "What did you think?"

"I wasn't sure. No one is wearing a uniform."

Gordy laughed. "We got more important things to do than wear uniforms. We wear them for each court of honor, but not for camping, rock climbing, hiking, or anything fun."

I smiled when I heard Gordy say that. My boys were farm boys. They worked hard all week, and scouting was their break from work. I knew that some people would frown at me for not insisting uniforms be worn at every activity, but I learned long ago to assess the importance of my battles. Some were worth fighting and some were not, and to me, there were more important rules requiring a line to be drawn.

David joined us for the evening's activities, and he seemed to enjoy himself. I was teaching the boys winter survival skills, and we were talking about how to safely build and use a snow cave.

"Do you guys really go camping in winter?" David asked.

"Of course," Gordy replied. "We have the Klondike Derby

coming up the weekend after this one. A guy is only half a man if he can't survive outside in the winter."

David looked doubtful, so I explained that if a person was prepared, winter camping was not only safe, but could be a lot of fun.

We ended the evening with a rousing game of basketball, something we usually did as a reward for the boys' diligence while I taught them. When we finished, I went with David to his home to visit with his mother about getting him registered.

David's mom, Leanna, welcomed me with a big smile. "I'm so glad that David has found a scout troop to join," she said. "He was active in his troop in California and has seemed lost without them."

"We're glad to have him with us," I said, handing her the registration paperwork to fill out. "We are a very active troop, and I think he will have a lot of fun."

She started filling out the paperwork as she continued to speak. "In California, I think they went camping every single month."

I nodded. "Yes, we do, too."

She laughed. "Of course, not in the winter."

"But they do," David said. "They are going camping a week from Friday."

Suddenly Leanna's smile disappeared. She picked up the paper and slammed it into my chest. "That's stupid. It is below zero out there! I'm not letting my son go camping in this cold."

"But Mom . . . " David started to complain.

"No!" she answered. "And that is final!" She then turned to me. "I can't believe you could be so irresponsible!"

"Scouting is about preparedness and survival," I answered. "We train the boys to survive in cold like this. They need to learn to deal with it because this is where they live. What will happen if your son is caught out somewhere without learning those skills?"

58

She continued to silently glare at me, so I continued. "I will be with them, and I promise that the boys will be fine. That's what we prepare them for."

Leanna looked at her son's pleading face, then at me, and, reluctantly, she signed. But as I was leaving, I heard her whisper to him, "I think we should be careful. I still think anyone who would take boys winter camping might be kind of crazy."

What's in a Nickname?

I went to the funeral of a friend this month. Though we will miss him, the funeral was not depressing, but was, instead, a celebration of the good life he lived. Steve faced his many trials in life with humor, energy, and a constant smile. He has been an inspiration to many, including me, and his goodness and that of his wonderful wife and children, have been a blessing to our community.

I knew quite a bit about Steve. But as his two children told the events of his life, I learned even more about pranks he had pulled and the funny things he had done. And as I listened, I thought of another story he once told me.

I had always had a great curiosity about how Steve got his nickname. Everyone called him "Cookie" and for many years, that was all I had known him by. But one day, after I finally learned his real name, I asked him how he had happened upon his strange moniker.

Steve grinned his big grin and laughed. "Well, it's really kind of embarrassing." He laughed again and then told me the story.

He said that when he was a small boy, he was at church and grew bored with Sunday School. He and some friends slipped out a back door and made their way to a store called Joey's Market that was a couple of blocks away.

Steve was a good boy, but church had gone a long time, so by the time he got to Joey's Market he was hungry. But he didn't have any money, and the things in the store were so tempting. He browsed up and down the aisles, and then his eyes settled on some chocolate-covered graham cracker cookies. Those were by far his favorite.

He looked around to see if anyone was watching, and then, carefully, he took them and tried to sneak out of the store.

But his actions had not gone unnoticed. Joey had seen him. Joey caught Steve red-handed, and Steve knew he was in trouble. Joey could have called the police, but he was a good man, and he felt that a run-in with the law could do more harm than good to a young boy. He had devised his own way of dealing with the waywardness of impish children. Joey had become a master at using peer pressure for rehabilitating boys from the errors of their delinquency.

Joey gathered all of Steve's friends around, and he told them what Steve had done. That alone was enough to make Steve never want to shoplift again. But to guarantee that that would always be the case, Joey, pointing to Steve, said to all of the other boys, "From now on, we will call him 'Cookie' to help him remember this day."

All of the other boys laughed and agreed. And just as Joey suggested, the other boys truly did make sure that Steve never forgot it. And that was how "Cookie" became Steve's nickname.

Steve was such a great man — kind, caring, and always willing to help others. So as he finished the story, I laughed. "Well, I guess Joey's means of reformation worked on you."

Steve grinned sheepishly. "You think that's funny, huh? Well, I wasn't the only one he worked his reformation on."

I laughed. "Oh, really?"

Steve nodded. "How do you think Hershey Henderson got his name?"

It's All About Intimidation

Jerry was trying to persuade his friend Steve to join the wrestling team. "You would be a natural at it," Jerry said. "You're quick and you're smart. Besides, we don't really have anyone in your weight class."

"But I'm going to be a sophomore, and I've never wrestled before," Steve replied. "I'd be going up against guys that are older and have wrestled most of their lives."

"I think that wrestling is not as much about skill and experience as it is about getting inside your opponent's head," Jerry said.

"What do you mean?" Steve asked.

"It's all a game of intimidation," Jerry replied.

"Look at me," Steve said. "Do I look intimidating?"

"It's not really how a person looks," Jerry replied. "It's more in how they act."

That really intrigued Steve. He had already shown talent in football, and the thought of taking on the challenge of wrestling fascinated him. The thought of playing mind games with an opponent made it irresistible.

Steve showed up at practice, and Coach was happy to have him add some depths to the middle weights. And even though Jerry weighed quite a bit more, Steve and Jerry worked out together so Jerry could coach Steve on the finer points of the mental game.

When it came time for the first match of the season, Steve and Jerry had things all worked out. Jerry already had a reputation as a tough wrestler and was well known by the opposing team. When they went to warm up on the mat, Jerry and Steve made it look like Steve was really whipping him. The two knew it was working as the opposing team members were pointing at them and whispering among themselves.

When they finished with their warmup, Jerry walked over to the opposing team and went to the wrestler Steve would be wrestling. "Hey. Be careful wrestling him," Jerry said, pointing to Steve. "He can be a bit dangerous."

"What do you mean?" Steve's opponent asked.

Jerry leaned close, glanced around nervously, and spoke in a whisper as if he was afraid someone might hear him. "Look, I shouldn't be telling you this. But he was recently released from lockup for beating up a bunch of guys."

"Really?" Steve's opponent asked.

Jerry nodded. "Yeah. Don't let his size fool you. He's mean. I hear there were six of them, and he took the whole bunch."

"Thanks for telling me," Steve's opponent said.

Jerry nodded again. "You're welcome. I just happen to know that he's out to take revenge on anybody and everybody for being stuck in jail, and I just don't want anyone getting hurt."

As Jerry turned and headed back to his team bench, he couldn't hold back his smile. But it was even harder for Steve. As he looked across the gym and saw Jerry coming back with a big grin on his face, he still had to keep his composure and glare at his opponent.

As the night proceeded, Steve kept his glare fixed. Just before his match, he looked to make sure he had his opponent's attention. He then took a raw egg, cracked it on his own teeth, and dropped the contents into his mouth. He swallowed it, sneered at his opponent, and threw the egg shell into his mouth. He deliberately chewed them up and swallowed, and his reputation was fixed.

But he also learned that night that egg shells are hard on the digestive system.

An Instrument of Embarrassment

Steve had a sharp mind and an ear for music that few people experience. But he lacked something that almost all other musicians quickly master. He could not read music. He had never needed to. His good friend, John, always sat by him and would show him the positions on the trombone and how to play the notes within them for each piece of music. Steve, with his sharp mind, would learn quickly and never forget.

Every time they received a new song, he would have it memorized in only a few days simply by watching John. Then, while everyone else was fumbling along while reading from the scores on their music stands, he would simply play it from memory. Of course, he didn't want the teacher to know he couldn't read music, so when the others turned the pages of their music, he would follow their lead and continue his charade.

The band teacher never caught on, and he was duly impressed that when the others were dead without their music, Steve could jump in and play as if he was improvising. The teacher marveled at Steve's abilities, and Steve soon earned first chair in the trombone section.

But with first position came the nomination by his teacher to be part of the state honor band. Not going was simply not an option. Turning it down was unheard of. Steve grew nervous about it, knowing that John had not been nominated. He went to his teacher and asked him if John could go, too. He said that John was the one who had encouraged him and helped him become what he was, and he didn't feel he could go without him. The teacher thought it was just a matter of a close, supportive friendship, and he agreed to nominate John as well.

John was a good musician, but he didn't have Steve's ear or knack for picking up the music. They were given the music ahead of time, and John showed Steve how to play it. It wasn't long before Steve had it mastered, though John, for all of his musical ability, struggled with the difficult passages.

The time came for the two friends to join the other nominees and travel to the big event. A famous master teacher had come to conduct the band. He would teach the students during the day and then direct them in what was to be an outstanding evening concert.

Each group of instrumentalists lined up to play a few bars, after which they were seated according to how well the instructor felt they did. Steve, having all of the music memorized, played flawlessly when it was his turn. The maestro smiled and put Steve into first position for the trombones. His chair was the seat nearest the conductor, most visible to the audience. John didn't do as well and was seated far back in the middle of the group. Though Steve couldn't read the music, with John's help, he had marked the pages so he knew what to play at any point the director would have them come in.

The day went well. Steve played flawlessly all day and drew great praise from the conductor. He began to feel like he was invincible. He might even have been just a bit arrogant.

Once they had finished all of the rehearsals, they took a break before the concert. When they gathered again, and it came time to start, the auditorium was full. Steve smiled confidently. Then, just as they were ready to begin, the conductor turned to the audience and said, "And now, we will ask our lead trombonist to give us an A to tune the band."

He then turned to Steve and waved his baton. Steve froze. The conductor frowned and spoke to him, "Steve, please give us an A."

Steve's heart started to pound. And then he remembered John. Trying not to attract too much attention, he turned and desperately looked for him. Just as the conductor's patience was expiring, Steve saw John. John grinned and gave Steve the needed signal.

Steve turned back to the director and produced a clear, crisp A as he humbly realized an appreciation for the value of a good, loyal friend.

I went to a college reunion and was excited to see a former roommate there. Beside him was a beautiful lady, and behind them trailed four cute children.

I walked over to him and punched him in the arm. "They'll let anybody come to one of these things, won't they?"

He turned, and seeing me, his eyes grew wide. Jed punched me back. "I guess they will, because you're here."

I laughed, and as we shared our delight in seeing each other, our wives and children came up beside us. We did introductions, and then my wife asked them, "So how did you two meet?"

Pamela, Jed's wife, smiled. "It's a long story."

At college, Pamela was roommates with Jed's cousin, Sally. It was the first time the two girls had met, but they hit it off immediately. They did everything together and soon became close friends. As the year went on, Sally realized that since it was Pamela's senior year, she would be moving on and it was unlikely that their friendship would stay as strong.

That was when she hit on a plan. All she had to do was to get Jed and Pamela to marry, and then she and Pamela could be together at every family reunion. She approached Jed about asking Pamela out, but he would have none of it. He told her he didn't go out with girls he didn't know, and, besides, he had heard horror stories about people setting relatives up on blind dates.

She then talked to Pamela about asking Jed over for cookies or something.

"You are a great cook and you would really like him," Sally said.

But Pamela was too shy and felt that would be too forward. Sally threw out some more ideas to Jed and Pamela, but it was just making things worse. She even tried to get Jed to come over and visit so she could just happen to introduce the two of them. But Jed had grown wary of her motives and always found an excuse.

But one day, as she was visiting with him, he started coughing. "Are you ill?" she asked.

"Oh, just a little bit of a cold," Jed answered. "Nothing to worry about."

But suddenly Sally had an idea. As soon as she got back to her apartment, she waited until she knew Pamela was entering the room, and then she grabbed the phone from the receiver.

"Oh, Mom, I'm so worried about Jed," she said into it. "I wish I could make him dinner or something to help him feel better." She then went on, speaking into the phone, explaining how Jed was on death's doorstep.

Pamela, who had a big heart, couldn't help but overhear. She finally felt she had to help. "I don't see any reason we couldn't make him dinner," she said.

Sally turned to her. "But the way I cook, I might kill him."

"I could help," Pamela said.

"Oh, would you?" Sally said, hanging up the phone without thinking. Pamela stared at it, and Sally realized her mistake. "Oh, the phone. Uh, Mom heard you, and had to run, saying she'd let us deal with it."

Pamela trustingly believed her, and they set about making dinner. Pamela was an excellent cook and made some homemade bread. When it was done, they heated up some chicken noodle soup from a can, and headed out to deliver it.

When they arrived, Jed answered the door. Sally was quick to tell him that when Pamela heard he was sick, she insisted on making him some homemade bread and soup. Although Pamela was a bit confused and Jed was surprised by the attention, the smell of the hot bread broke down his defenses. He invited them in, and Sally suggested that there was enough they could all share. But just as they were starting to eat, Sally suddenly remembered she had a chemistry lab.

After she left, the silence between Jed and Pamela was awkward. But then he cut into the bread, and the aroma filled the air. His compliment on it warmed Pamela's heart, and soon they were talking and laughing together as they ate.

"And," Jed laughed, "later we learned that Sally didn't even have chemistry. But with great food like that, I was hooked, and she got her best friend as a cousin."

In the Big City

"Dad," my son said from the back of the van, "you need to go faster. Everyone is passing us."

He was right. The cars whizzed by us as though we had stopped to set up camp and put up our tent in the middle of the interstate.

Even my wife joined in. "You know, they can give you a ticket for going too slow."

I looked at my speedometer. I was already going ten miles over the speed limit. I could just see a police officer pulling me over. "Hey, Buddy. I'm going to have to give you a ticket for impeding traffic. You were only going 75 in the 65 mile-per-hour zone."

I thought that would look good in a court of law. However, I did try to speed up and at least keep up with traffic a little better because I was getting a lot of dirty looks from the other motorists.

We were taking my college-age daughter to a university hours from where we lived, and we had to drive through a big city to get there. The problem, I realized, is that I am a country boy through and through. I am not used to big city traffic. I don't care for someone pulling in front of me when he can barely squeeze his car in between my front bumper and the rear bumper of the car in front of me. I don't care for a car so close behind me that if I hit my brakes its passengers will be sitting next to me in the front seat of my car changing my radio station.

I'm used to the wide-open space. Our house is tucked into a small country lane, and we seldom see a car go by. When we do, everyone runs to the window to see who it is. Most of the time it's someone who is lost, whose GPS can't even figure out where they are.

I have had some of my big city relatives tease me for the

lifestyle I have chosen for myself and my family. I have wondered at times if I should have raised my family in a big city. I have had job offers from some large companies, but I always turned them down because I like the slower pace of my life, and I enjoy teaching students at the small, rural university where I work. But I have often wondered if my children have missed out on some of the wonders of city life, like Walmarts the size of New Jersey, traffic jams that are made by cars and not herds of sheep, and shopping malls the size of the town where I grew up.

Though I describe the city from my point of view, there truly are some wonderful things that are not found outside of a big city. In the city many things are bigger and there are more of them. There are more museums, more theaters, and more of many other cultural events.

As we came up over the ridge and started to drop down into the valley on the other side, the acidic smell of car exhaust hit us so hard it made our eyes water.

"What is that horrible smell?" my four-year-old asked. "It smells like someone ran over thousands of skunks."

I laughed at her farm-girl description and then tried to explain to her what it was. "Well," she replied, "I'm glad I don't live here. I'll be glad to get home."

I thought about the day before we left. We went out to our garden as a family and picked raspberries, sweet corn, and peas, and then we dug new fresh potatoes. It was all for a special dinner for my daughter before she left. The birds sang around us, and the frogs added a strong bass. The smell on the breeze was that of the wheat harvest in full swing.

As my thoughts returned to the present, I smiled at my four year old. "I'll be glad to get home, too."

But I realized that I occasionally like to visit a city, and I am glad that there are lots of different people in the world, each with their own idea of what makes life good.

A Visit to the College President

It was my second year of college, and I was attending a religious university. As with any such university, there were strong guidelines for admittance. These included modest dress, proper grooming, honesty, and a strong moral code. Before I came, a paper had to be signed that I, on my honor, would obey these guidelines. I was happy to sign it and even happier to live it. I enjoyed that type of environment and the association with other young people who lived those same standards.

But one day I received a call that surprised me. My roommate, Bryce, answered the phone, and the lady told him she was calling from the Honor Office and needed to speak to me. Bryce was shocked that I would receive such a call. He handed over the phone and then quickly informed all of my other roommates about it.

Immediately they all gathered around, staring at me, making me very self-conscious. I said hello into the phone, and the lady on the other end spoke very businesslike. "Mr. Howard, this is Becky from the Honor Office. We have been informed that you are in violation of the school honor code."

My heart started to pound, and I could hardly breathe. I thought hard, trying to remember something I might have done that was against the rules, but I couldn't think of anything. "What?" was all I could say.

"It is inappropriate to discuss something of this great magnitude over the phone," Becky said. "We need you to come in."

"When?" I asked.

"Something like this needs to be dealt with immediately. Are you free right now?"

"Uh, yeah. I think I could come."

"This particular matter is of grave concern," she said. "We are not going to be dealing with this ourselves. You need to talk directly to the college president."

"The college president?" I gasped.

"Yes, the president," she replied. "May I inform him that you are on your way and will be there shortly?"

"Yes, Ma'am."

"Thank you," she replied. "He will be expecting you."

When I hung up the phone, my roommates were all staring at me. Although they had heard only one end of the conversation, that, along with the shocked look on my face, was enough.

"I have to meet with the president!"

"Wow!" Bryce said. "What did you do?"

"Nothing," I said, but by their smirks, I knew they didn't believe me.

The walk to the president's office was a long one. The wait in the reception area was worse. Finally, the president came out and ushered me into his office. He spoke sternly to me, speaking to me about rules and the importance of having and obeying them. I fidgeted a lot, wondering when he would finally tell me what violation I had been called in for.

But he never did. Instead he stopped, and glared at me, so I timidly asked, "Will you please tell me what it was that I did?"

His expression remained unchanged. "As if you didn't know," he growled.

He stared sternly at me for another brief moment. Then he suddenly started to smile and then to laugh. He laughed and laughed. Finally he stopped and wiped his eyes. "You ought to see your face," he said.

He then reached over and hit a button on his phone. "Iris," he said, "I think you need to come in here."

With that, my aunt came in the door. I instantly remembered

that she was the president's personal secretary, even though I had never seen her in that capacity. She pulled me into her arms and gave me a hug. "You know, you never come up to see me, so I thought an April Fool's joke was in order."

I smiled, and then I laughed, remembering that my roommates didn't know anything yet, and it was still April first. Maybe I could think of some way to turn this into a joke on them.

The Great Bean Experiment

John, one of my roommates, had never learned to cook. His family had always had a lot of money and servants. But just before he came to college, his family had had a major setback and lost almost everything. He not only had nonexistent culinary skills, but now he had very little money.

He had spent some time in South America and determined that the best and cheapest thing to eat would be beans. He said he liked beans. So every other day he put a huge pot of beans on to cook. Sometimes he ate them three times per day.

Unfortunately, beans affected John in the same way that they affect many people. He became a methane factory with production that would put a natural gas company to shame. Fortunately, I did not share his bedroom, but those who did were desperate. They claimed they had to open their window at night, even in the winter, or they would all suffocate by morning.

John didn't like to make his bed, so he, instead, only used a sleeping bag. One night, David, who slept in the bunk below John, was having a nightmare. He dreamed he was in a war, and the enemy was using mustard (and bean) gas, making it necessary for him to search for a gas mask. When he awoke and realized he really did need one, he hit on an idea. He quietly climbed out of his bed and zipped John's sleeping bag up to his neck.

The next morning, when David got up, he told us his story and claimed his night had been much better after that. However, he said he didn't know what John would do once he woke up. We didn't have to wait long. We knew the moment John unzipped his sleeping bag because a sudden blast of air, as rancid as that of any skunk, flooded the apartment.

Our eyes started to water, and everyone started coughing

even as I ran to open the door and David worked to open a window. John came out yawning, seemingly unaware of the aroma that followed him or the distress it was causing us.

From then on, every night after John went to sleep, David would quietly zip John's sleeping bag up tight. This made it bearable for the others in that bedroom. But each morning when John woke and unzipped it, it was as if a high pressure septic line had burst into our apartment.

No one wanted to offend John, nor did we know how to approach him about it. Many of us tried. We even offered to share our food, trying to get him onto another diet, but he always said he liked the way the beans made him feel and the energy they gave him.

"High octane gas," Bryce whispered to me. "Great for internal combustion, but deadly for those behind the exhaust pipe."

No matter how many hints we dropped, nor how hard we tried, he never seemed to catch on. He always thought we were talking about someone else.

Finally, we could take it no more. So one day, when John was in class, we held an apartment council.

"I have an idea," Bryce said. "Let's pack up his stuff and put it outside and lock the door."

I shook my head. "John doesn't have much money, and he has paid to stay here just like the rest of us."

"I was only teasing," Bryce replied, though I'm not sure he was.

"Well, let's look at the facts," David said. "We know John won't eat anything but beans, and beans give him gas. So the only option I see is that we need to change them for something else."

"Like a twenty-year, Rip Van Winkle sleeping potion," Steve said.

Suddenly, Bryce snapped his fingers. "I've got it! I'm taking chemistry, and we are always talking about PH balance and all that stupid stuff. Well, for once, maybe I can find a use for all of that nonsense. There has got to be something that will counteract those beans."

And with that, the greatest chemistry experiment in the history of mankind was launched.

The Great Chemistry Experiment

John was our roommate at college. He was not a great cook and had little money, and for that reason he decided he could live totally on beans. The problem was that they created in him an atomic cloud of methane that was driving the rest of us to near suffocation.

The situation was becoming desperate, and the rest of us held an apartment council to see if we could come up with a way to neutralize what we called the "John effect."

"My home is near an oil refinery," Steve said. "They have a tall pipe that always has a fire on it, burning off the excess, unwanted gases. Why don't we do the same thing? We could keep some candles burning in our apartment."

"I don't think that is a good idea," David replied. "The pipe at the oil refinery is outside, not inside. I'm afraid if we had a gas buildup and someone lit a match, we could blow ourselves to the next county."

"How about we rig an exhaust fan in the window in John's bedroom?" Bryce suggested.

"May I remind you," David said, "that I share that bedroom. It's winter, and I already have the window open a slight bit. If we open it much more, we'll freeze to death."

"Well, we've got to do something," Bryce said. "I don't think there's a gas we've used in our chemistry class that is as potent, and we still use an exhaust fan in there."

Suddenly, Bryce's eyes lit up — an indication that he had just had an idea. "You know what?" he said. "My chemistry class is the answer."

"How so?" Steve asked.

"Well, we have been talking about acids and bases and how they neutralize each other because they somehow counteract each other's carbons. Well, John is about as carbon as anything can get. All we have to do is find out if the gas is an acid or a base and then neutralize him."

We were skeptical, but Bryce couldn't wait to talk to his teacher. It was the first time I had seen him excited about going to class. Later that day he came back to report. "Guys, my teacher says methane is an acid, so all we have to do is figure a base we can use that won't kill John in the process."

I had done a lot of mechanic work, and I had the perfect solution. "A car battery is full of acid," I said. "When we want to clean one, we use a mixture of baking soda and water."

"Perfect," Bryce said. "Let's all pool our money and I will buy some baking soda."

We all chipped in, and Bryce left. When he returned he had the biggest bag of baking soda I had ever seen. It said it was twelve pounds. "Are you sure you need that much?" I asked.

"I'm not leaving anything to chance," he replied.

John's four-gallon pot was half full of beans and water, simmering on the stove. Bryce took the lid off and poured in a cup of baking soda. He looked at the small cup, then at the big bag, then at the pot.

"I say if a person is going to do an experiment, he needs to do it right," Bryce said. Then, before anyone could stop him, he poured most of the bag into the pan.

We were lucky the pot was only half full, or it would have boiled over. It almost did anyway.

"That much soda will taste terrible," I told him. "John will know."

"The way he cooks," Bryce answered, "he'll only know if it causes him to explode."

That night when John sat down to eat his beans, everyone was nonchalantly gathered around. He buried them in ketchup, as usual, and started to eat.

"How are the beans?" I asked.

John shrugged. "Same as usual. Why?"

"Oh," I replied, "just curious."

But the experiment seemed to work. For the first time, the air in our apartment was breathable. And from then on, if anyone asked us why one cupboard was stocked full of baking soda, we simply said it was for an ongoing chemistry experiment.

It's the Simple Things That Matter Most

The end of the semester was busy with students complaining about their grades and wanting to know if there was any way they could make up for their lack of diligence during the semester. I was feeling quite tired and sat down in my office chair to rest.

That was when I noticed an envelope that had been slipped under my door. I picked it up and opened it, and a letter fell out. I started to read.

"Dear Professor Howard, I am Richard Hampton. It has been a couple of years since I took your calculus class, so you probably don't remember me."

I paused and smiled as the memory came back. It started in a very basic algebra class, one that students usually take in high school. Richard was quiet. He sat in the back of the class, head always down, never making eye contact with anyone.

When the students took their first test, Richard failed. I marked his grade on his test and was just ready to stick it back in the pile when something made me pause. As the thought of Richard filled my mind, so did the thought of a little boy back in grade school. It was a boy who was incessantly teased, had no friends, and was unable to read. I was that boy, and what saved me was a teacher who cared.

I thought about it for a moment and then wrote a note on his test asking him to come see me. I wasn't sure he would, but the next day there was a timid knock on my door. When I opened it, Richard was standing there, his eyes looking down. "You wanted to see me?"

I offered him a seat, and he sat, still looking at the floor. "Richard," I said, "your test bothers me more than any other test I've graded this semester."

He looked up in surprise before quickly lowering his eyes

again. "Why?" he asked.

"Because," I answered, "you show great ability in your work. I know you can do better than this. I can see it in your logical analysis of the problems."

He looked at me, and his shock was obvious. "You really think I have the ability?"

"I know you do," I said. "Oh, it might be hard work, but you can't let that deter you."

"But there are things in class I don't quite understand."

"So ask."

"But what if everyone laughs?"

I leaned forward in my chair, up close to him. "Let them laugh. When your grade is higher than theirs because you understand, then it's you who can laugh. And someday, when you are a millionaire, you remember that our department could use a math scholarship."

I smiled, and he laughed, the first positive emotion I had seen from him. He totally changed after that. He participated in class and ended the semester with a high B. He took college algebra and calculus from me, receiving As in both. But then he was done with his math and disappeared from my life.

I turned back to his letter and continued to read.

"I don't know if you knew that my mother passed away when I started high school. My father remarried, and my stepmother hated me. She criticized everything I did, and I thought I could do nothing right. My grades went down, and I barely graduated. I wanted to be an engineer, but my stepmother told me I would never amount to anything and could never make it through college.

"Unfortunately, I believed her, especially after failing your first exam, and I thought I would drop out. But I read your note and decided to come see you. You will never know how much of a difference it made in my life just to know that someone believed in me.

"I couldn't leave without saying thank you and letting you know that I graduate tomorrow with honors in electrical engineering. You are the best teacher I have ever had."

As I finished the letter, I smiled to myself. I had really never done much more than the simple visit with Richard that day. But I realized that sometimes in life, it's the simple things that matter most.

Crossed Wires

When I was in high school, I had a little pickup that I drove everywhere. But one day it started smelling like burning plastic. After further inspection, I found that some of the wiring had shorted and melted.

My dad had me leave it at his shop. He owned a farm business and sold tractors, combines, and any other type of farm equipment a person could possibly want. He said that he would have one of the mechanics who worked for him put a new wiring harness on it.

The problem was that most farm equipment were big diesel machines. I expressed my concern to my father, but he assured me that the wiring was the same.

My dad told the mechanic that he wanted it finished by Friday. I would be traveling to a wrestling meet in Salmon, a distance that took more than three hours to travel one way on the bus. I wouldn't arrive back at the school until about 1:00 in the morning, and my parents hoped I would be able to drive myself home.

On the morning of the meet, my dad drove me to his shop so I could drive my pickup to the school. It wasn't too far to the school, but there was one right turn and one left turn. When I made the right turn and turned on my blinker, it didn't blink, but I thought nothing of it other than to think the mechanic might have missed that wire.

When I went to make the left turn and turned on the blinker, the horn honked. Once again, I didn't think anything of it, other than to think I must have inadvertently hit the horn. I parked the pickup and went to class.

At noon we left for Salmon. The meet went well, and I won my match, but it was a long way home, and I was exhausted when we arrived. Three of my friends asked if they could catch a ride home, and I agreed.

We all stuffed into the little cab, and I started the engine. I then reached up and pulled on the lights. The lights didn't come on, but the radio did, and it was so loud it nearly blew us out of the cab. I instinctively reached up to turn the radio down, but when I turned the knob, the windshield wipers started going instead. Suddenly, I realized I had a problem.

The radio was still blaring, and everyone was covering their ears, so I reached up and shut the light switch off. Immediately a wonderful stillness filled the air. I reached up and carefully turned on the light switch, and once again the radio blared. I quickly shut it off again.

"What's wrong with your pickup?" Curly asked.

"My dad's mechanic just replaced the wiring harness," I replied. "I think he must have gotten some wires crossed."

"Some?" Curly said, reaching up and turning on the radio and watching the wipers go. "I think the mechanic has his wires crossed."

Remembering that morning, I reached up and hit the left signal. The horn immediately honked.

"What are you doing?" Lenny asked.

"Trying to find the lights," I told him.

"Here, let me help," he replied.

He hit the windshield wiper button, but we didn't see anything. Donald got out to check things from the outside, and when we hit the wiper button again, he yelled that the brake lights came on.

"Wow!" Lenny said. "This is fun."

Curly reached out and hit the horn, and the left signal blinked outside. I hit the brakes, and the hazard lights started to flash. I hit the heater fan switch, and the right signal blinked. Finally, Lenny hit the right blinker and the lights came on. Once we had lights, Donald piled back in.

"If everyone can help me remember what does what, maybe we can get ourselves home," I said. And with that, I pushed on my horn to signal a left turn so I could pull out from the curb.

Driving With Crossed Wires

After arriving home from a wrestling meet at one o'clock in the morning, my friends asked for a ride. We soon realized that the mechanic who had worked on the wiring in my pickup had mixed things up. However, once we knew what each switch did, we felt confident we could still make our way home.

I was really tired, but I knew if I pulled the light switch on to turn the radio on, it would blast us out of the pickup. But then I remembered that the light switch was also tied to the dash dimmer. I pulled the light switch and the radio blared, but then I quickly turned the knob for the dash light dimmer and, indeed, the radio volume decreased. Unfortunately, the station the mechanic had put it on was not one I liked, but I couldn't figure out how to change it.

I held the right blinker on, so I would have headlights as we traveled. As we approached the first stop sign, I hit the wiper switch to turn on the brake lights, and then I pressed the horn to turn on my left blinker. I then turned off the wiper switch to shut off my brake lights and we continued on our way. When we pulled up to the next stop sign I did a similar thing, except I reached over and clicked on the heater fan switch to signal a right turn.

All of my friends who were traveling with me would remind me what each switch did. As soon as we turned the next corner, I noticed a car was following us. After we stopped at the next stop sign and started to pull out again, my rearview mirror was suddenly filled with red and blue flashing lights.

Lenny laughed. "I can't wait to hear you try to talk yourself out of this one."

The police officer came up to my window. "So where are you guys coming from?" he asked.

"We came back from a wrestling meet and just arrived back at the school," I told him. "We are heading home."

"Well," he said, "you are probably wondering why I pulled

you over. I want to know why you turn on your flashers every time you come to a stop."

My friends tried to muffle their laughs as I spoke. "You see, Officer," I replied. "My pickup was just rewired by a mechanic, and he crossed some wires. I didn't know about it until we got home from the meet."

The officer looked doubtful. "I see. Would you mind demonstrating?"

"The light switch turns the radio on and off," I said, and I pushed it to off. Immediately the radio went silent. "The hazard lights turn on the heater fan," I said, as I demonstrated.

"The radio button turns on the wipers," Lenny said, reaching up and turning the radio dial. The wipers started going back and forth. Then, for some reason, Lenny turned the channel dial, and the wipers sped up. He turned it back, and they slowed down. He started laughing as he continued turning them up and down.

I slapped his hand away. "Stop it! You're not helping!"

I turned back to the officer, who was struggling to keep a straight face. "So," he said, "what turns the flashers on?"

"They are connected to the brake," I replied, pushing the brake pedal to show him.

"So why do the brake lights turn on, too?" he asked.

"Because I turned them on to let people know I was slowing," I replied. "They are tied to the windshield wiper switch." I demonstrated, and the officer didn't even try to hold a straight face. "Seriously, sir," I said, "I will take it back first thing tomorrow."

He nodded. "I suppose you can all get home safely tonight. I'm going to let you go. But you make sure you get it fixed. Driving with all those crossed wires is quite dangerous."

"Thank you, sir," I said.

"No, thank you," he replied. "I think you just helped me win the department pool for the best story of the month."

And with that, he laughed as he walked back to his patrol car.

Logic

I was walking down the hall to my office when I heard someone call my name. I turned and saw a young couple coming quickly toward me. As they came closer, I recognized them. They had been my students a couple of years earlier. They had worked in the same group, and I had thought they kind of liked each other. As they hurried toward me, hand in hand, it was quite obvious I was right.

When they reached me, Sheila blurted out, "Professor Howard, do you remember us?"

I nodded. "I sure do." I looked and saw a ring on her finger. "Did you two . . . ?"

She didn't even let me finish, speaking as she held her ring hand up. "Yes, we got married. Almost a year ago."

"That is really exciting," I replied.

"We first met in your Math for the Real World class," Tom said. "We became study partners."

"And we did quite well," Sheila added, "except for logic. The logic section blew both of us away."

"Yeah," Tom said. "Logic just didn't work for us. We studied hard on it and neither of us could get it. But we did well on everything else, and we finished with okay grades."

"Logic can be difficult for some people," I said.

Tom shrugged. "I don't see why it's part of the class. Logic just isn't important in real life."

"Well, anyway," Sheila interjected, "we were on our way to see you just now. We wanted to let you know that we had married."

"In addition," Tom said, "we wanted to tell you that we are expecting our first baby."

"That is exciting," I replied. "Congratulations!"

Sheila smiled. "The ultrasound shows that the baby is going

to be a boy. Tom and I have talked about it, and we think we ought to do something to remember that we first met in a math class. We think our baby's middle name ought to be something mathematical."

"We considered Pythagoras," Tom said, "but Sheila thinks that's too old fashioned."

"Tom was thinking of using a math term," Sheila said. "Maybe something derived from a word like addition or multiplication or something."

"Do you have any good ideas?" Tom asked.

I shook my head. "I'm afraid I'm not very good with things like that. If you used something I came up with, I'm sure your son would end up hating me for the rest of his life."

"If you think of something, I hope you'll let us know," Sheila said. "This baby was kind of a surprise, so we don't have as much time to consider a name as we would have liked."

"The baby was a surprise?" I asked.

Tom nodded. "Yeah. When we got married, Sheila's doctor talked to her all about contraceptives and helped her decide on the best kind. But obviously it didn't work."

"And we know it wasn't our fault," Sheila said, "because Tom was careful to take the birth control pills exactly as the doctor prescribed them for me."

"Tom took them?" I questioned in surprise.

Sheila nodded. "Yeah. I took the pills for a little while, but they made me sick. So Tom was kind enough to take them instead." She then turned to him and smiled. "The medicine made him queasy, too, but he is such a great guy that he was kind enough to keep taking them anyway." Tom looked embarrassed at her compliment, and I tried hard not to smile.

As they turned to leave, Sheila said, "Thanks for such a great math class. But you still ought to see if the math department would take the logic part out. It's so useless."

"Yeah," Tom agreed.

"And," Sheila added, "if you think of a mathematical middle name for us, feel free to let us know."

I told them I would, but as they headed on their way, I knew one thing I wouldn't suggest for a middle name–logic.

Happiness and Freedom

I was living in a community that decided to run a memorial exhibit on the Holocaust. I felt it would be a good learning experience for me and my family. When we reached the exhibit, we each randomly drew a name according to our age and gender. We put on a tag with that name, and we were supposed to address each other accordingly. Through the exhibit we would learn things about the person's life.

My person was a man about my same age—early forties. He was married and had two little girls. He was a school teacher and was well-liked by his students and those who knew him. He and his family were taken right at the beginning of the Holocaust to Auschwitz. His wife and two daughters were killed almost immediately. He was healthy and strong, so he was not killed but was forced to work doing slave labor.

As we continued through the exhibit, my family and I began to relate with the people whose names we had, even feeling as if we were those people. We laughed at the things the person liked, enjoyed their talents and hobbies, and learned how they lived and what their daily routines were like. As their lives took tragic turns, we could almost feel the pain with them.

At one point during our journey, there was a man who had helped put the exhibit together. He was willing to answer questions, but I saw no one taking advantage of that opportunity. I decided to take some time to visit with him.

I asked him if he had had any personal experience with Holocaust. He nodded. "I was at Auschwitz. Most of my family died there, and I found myself feeling bitter and resentful, with my only thoughts being thoughts of vengeance. But then something happened. I noticed that there were prisoners there who were happy. I realized they were the ones who were able to make themselves free."

"Did they escape?" I asked.

"No. They made decisions for themselves, so that even when their liberty was taken away, their freedom was not."

"What's the difference between liberty and freedom?" I asked.

"Liberty is a person's ability to come and go as they choose. But freedom goes much deeper and comes from within. I watched as those men, even though they had no liberty, still chose to be free. While others could only dwell on their own personal misery, those men chose happiness. Some wrote happy stories, and some wrote inspired music, even if they wrote in nothing but the dirt on the ground or scratches on the wall. Others simply chose to help others, giving of themselves and even of their meager rations when they themselves were near starvation. Those men chose not to let their captors determine their happiness, their misery, nor their actions. Only they could determine what they would be, and they chose a positive attitude, even in the darkest abyss of prison and despite our inhumane treatment.

"I realized those men were truly free because their circumstances could not dictate who or what they would be. I made the determination that I also would find that freedom within myself. It was not easy, and at times, when a guard was especially vicious, I could feel myself slipping back into thoughts of revenge. But when I realized what was happening to me, I would work to force those thoughts out of my mind, even to the point I could almost forgive the unforgivable acts done by our captors."

"That seems so impossible," I said.

"It's not easy," he replied. "I don't think one in a thousand is able to find the fortitude to develop it in their lives. I know I never mastered it, but striving to that end did give me the strength and hope to endure, and I think it is what helped me to survive. And when the war was finally over, it helped me to go on with my life and put what had happened behind me."

As I finished the exhibit, I learned that after the person whose name I had was no longer of value to the Germans, he was killed. At first, a feeling of animosity came over me, but then I thought about what the man had told me, and I made a determination to do as he said.

I would choose happiness and freedom.

A Day of Fear and Thanksgiving

On Saturday, June 5, 1976, my younger sister came running out to where I was fixing a fence our cows had broken down. It was lunchtime, and I thought she might be coming to call me to come eat. But I quickly realized by the way she was running that something was wrong.

"Daris," she said, panting, her voice sounding panicked, "the radio said the Teton Dam broke and that St. Anthony has been destroyed!"

My parents and the rest of my brothers and sisters were in St. Anthony. I threw down my tools and raced back to the house. "What do we do?" she asked.

I decided we should try to call my father at his office. I called and he answered calmly.

"Dad, the radio said the Teton Dam broke and St. Anthony is under water!" I said.

He laughed. "I can tell you that I'm not treading water. I haven't seen or heard anything, but I'll check and learn what I can and call you back."

I waited for a while as we continued to listen to the radio. Dad didn't call, so after some time I tried to call him again. This time the phone was dead. My mind raced, trying to think of anything I could do. But just then, the radio announced that they were wrong and the water had not touched St. Anthony, but had cut through Wilford and turned toward Sugar City and Rexburg.

I had a lot of friends living in those areas, and my relief about the security of St. Anthony was quickly replaced by the fear of a possible loss of friends.

Suddenly the power went out. I searched desperately for a radio that ran on batteries but could not find one. Not knowing what was going on made us imagine the worst, and that was far worse than any bad news could be. My sister and I needed to know what was happening. Finally, I remembered that our old hay truck had a radio. I retrieved the key from a key hook, we made our way to the truck, and I turned on the radio.

We listened as KRXK continued to report the news. That station was in Rexburg, right in the main path of the flood waters. Still, they kept broadcasting, apparently with backup generators, until the last minute when they reported they were fleeing for safety on the Rexburg hill.

When the station went dead, I quickly turned the dial. Other stations were reporting the news, but what one would say would contradict the news from another. A measure of relief swept over us when our mother and our brothers and sisters drove into the yard in our old car. Still, we didn't know where Dad was, and those arriving didn't know either.

We sat in the old car most of the afternoon, listening to the radio. As evening came, my dad drove into the yard, followed by another car. Dad announced that we would have another family, whose home had been destroyed, staying with us for a few months.

As the other family climbed from their car, we counted seven young children along with the two parents. They, with the ten of our family who were still living at home, would make a full house.

We teenage boys spent the next few hours moving our belongings to the basement so the new family could have our rooms. The living room would be the boys' bedroom, and we would spend the summer sleeping on the living room floor.

We worked to rig a backup generator to be able to milk our cows and then worked until after dark to finish chores. The last news we heard that evening as we prepared for bed was that even though people were still missing, the number was small, and most people were accounted for.

As our two families knelt together before going to bed, even though there was a daunting task of rebuilding ahead of everyone in that valley, all we could think of was our gratitude that there was very little loss of life and that our families were safe.

We realized that nothing else really mattered.

The Most Important Wagon

After the Teton Dam broke and flooded the valley, everyone busily worked to help those who had been affected. My dad owned both a large farm and a business selling farm equipment, and the tractors were quickly put to use moving mountains of mud and debris. My oldest brothers ran those.

My brothers just older than me helped dig mud out of houses and do other cleanup work. I was in my mid-teens, and I was the youngest one who was still old enough to take on the farm work at home. While they were off helping, I was left milking cows, changing pipe, and fixing fence. At times, my dad would also have me come in and help do mechanic work at his farm business as the amount of repair work on damaged machinery was overwhelming for the workers. I really wanted to be out helping those affected by the flood like my brothers were, but my father said he needed me too much.

There was only one thing that I was able to do that made me feel a little like I was helping in the recovery effort. My mother was in charge of distributing the food that came to the local church building. When a big shipment arrived, she would call and tell me they needed my help. I would then unload truckloads of flour, sugar, and canned goods.

I was often up before five a.m. and worked until well after dark to keep up with the extra chores I needed to do while my brothers were gone. But each day, when they came home and told stories about who they had helped, I would feel less and less like my contributions were of any value. One day I could stand it no longer, and I begged my dad to let me go with them.

He smiled and asked, "Son, which wagon do you think is the most important wagon in the wagon train?"

I couldn't see what that had to do with anything, but I answered, "The first one. It's the one leading the way, showing everyone where to go."

He shook his head. "The first one is actually the second most important. The most important one is the last wagon, even though that is the one that no one ever hears about, and it is the one that gets everyone else's dust."

That seemed crazy to me. But my father explained. "When they choose those who will be in the last wagon, they look for the ones who are the bravest and most reliable. They have to watch over everyone. They must make sure no one is left behind. They have to help those who struggle or grow weary. They usually carry the greatest burden, having to deal with other people's challenges along with their own.

"But most importantly," my dad continued, "they must be willing to give their lives for everyone else. You see, if an attack comes, it will almost always come at the back of the wagon train. Those in the last wagon must be the ones who are always on guard and can hold off the attackers until the others have time to circle up and form a defense. Quite often, in so doing, those in the last wagon give their lives so that the others might live. And they usually do it with little or no recognition."

As I pondered this, my dad continued. "Right now, you are the last wagon. You are the one that picks up the pieces so your brothers can help others. I know that while they may be receiving praise for the great work they are doing, you receive almost no recognition at all. But without your efforts, they couldn't do it."

I thought a lot about that back then, and I have ever since. Now, when I am just a person in the choir and not the soloist, when I am the person in the play helping move the set, and I am not the star, or when I am the person on the committee doing the hard work while others receive the recognition, I simply remember the last wagon in the wagon train. And then I am okay with being the last wagon.

Frustration Turned to a Miracle

After the Teton Dam broke and water flooded the valley, we all worked long, hard hours to rebuild our lives, homes, and businesses. While my brothers often went out to help in the flood area, I was left home to take care of the chores there. My father also had me help the mechanics who worked at his farm equipment business.

On one particular day, I was helping to repair tractors damaged by the flood. While I was taking a short break, I heard my father's voice filled with excitement.

"John, I'm so glad to see you! I heard you were on the list of people still missing after the flood." My father called me over. "Daris, you remember John, don't you?"

John reached out his hand to shake mine. I reached mine out, but then I saw my hand was black with oil, and I laughed. "I don't think you want to shake my hand."

John grabbed my hand and shook it anyway. "I don't really care. Life is so good."

"You seem unusually happy," my father said.

"You remember how you heard I was on the missing list?" John asked. "Well, I truly was missing for a few days." He then went on to tell us his story.

He said that on the day of the flood he had been traveling from St. Anthony to Rexburg. On the old highway between the towns there was an overpass that went over some railroad tracks. As he came right to the flat part at the peak of the overpass, his car died. He thought maybe the angle coming up the overpass had drained the gas away from the intake hose in the tank, but in looking at his gas gauge, he knew the tank was too full for that.

He thought if he could just coast to the downhill slope he might be able to get it going again, but the car came to a complete stop some distance from where the slope turned downward. He thought there couldn't be a more inopportune place to be stopped since he would be blocking traffic. He was sure someone would soon come and help him push his car.

But no one came. The road seemed quieter than he had ever seen it. He knew a thing or two about cars, so he tried to restart it but had no luck. He was growing increasingly frustrated when the thought came to him that something strange was going on. Everything was deathly still. From his elevated view on the overpass, he couldn't see any vehicle moving anywhere.

The whole area was deserted. He was dumbfounded as to an explanation. Then, suddenly, he heard a roar. He looked to the east and saw a wall of water twenty feet high billowing toward him. As the water hit the overpass supports, the overpass vibrated underneath him, but it stood. He realized that if his car hadn't stopped where it had, he would have been killed.

He was trapped there for a couple of days. He had lots of time to think about how lucky he was. When he was finally rescued, he was hungry, thirsty, and tired, but he was okay.

Later, when things dried out enough for him to go back to the overpass, he walked up to his car, started it right up, and drove it off. As he finished his story, John spoke quietly. "It had never stalled before that day, and it has never stalled since."

He continued, speaking solemnly. "I've thought a lot about it since then. I hadn't really thought that there was much purpose or reason to life. Every day was just another day of work. But suddenly, all of that changed. As I sat on that overpass waiting for rescue, I thought about how I spent lots of time working but spent little time with my family. When my ordeal was over, I felt like I had been given another chance to reconsider what was most important to me, and I determined I would change."

After John left, my father turned to me and said, "John has always been a good man who loved his family, but perhaps we can take his lesson to heart and not get caught up in the thick of thin things."

And now, when I find myself busy with unimportant things, I remember John's story and it helps me put my life back into perspective.

What Students Learned in Math Class, 2014

Over the years, we have found that one of the students' greatest criticisms of any math class is their claim that they didn't learn anything. Therefore, as part of their final, I have the students list ten things that they have learned. These items can be anything at all in relation to the class. They are allowed to write their list ahead of time and bring it to the final if they want. Most observations are quite normal, but some make for interesting reading. Each year I list some of them, and here is this year's list.

1) I learned not to go to class hungry. You can't think.

2) I learned it is better to just do your homework than to keep worrying about doing it.

3) I learned some parts of math aren't as bad as I thought. Of course, I also learned that others are worse than I thought.

4) I learned that the guy sitting next to me smells amazing.

5) I learned that class was not meant for sleeping, but I can't seem to stay awake.

6) It is easy to remember what it is called when money is gaining because it is like a person getting fat so it is called come-pounding.

7) I learned that I always think I will get my work done over the weekend, but I never do.

8) I learned I wasn't good at math, only crunching numbers. I also learned that the two are different.

9) I learned that a girl in class that I don't like had a crush on me. Eww!

10) I learned that I hope my husband knows math because I sure don't.

11) The only thing I want for Christmas is a passing grade.

12) I learned that using your dollar on a fast food dollar menu is more useful than using it on the lottery. At least you get something for your dollar.

13) I learned that I should be listening in class and not drawing. But some of the examples Professor Howard uses in class give me some great inspiration for cool pictures.

14) I learned it isn't smart to take girls out that you take a class with. Something always goes wrong.

15) Threw (sic) this class I learned to present myself.

16) I learned that if I do my homework before the exam, then I am able to get a higher score on the test. Now I just need to figure out how to get myself to do the homework.

17) I learned to appreciate probability more. I used to really hate it. I actually still do, but at least I appreciate it more.

18) On the budget project, I thought that it would be okay to just work a minimum wage job. But after I worked through it and finished processing the numbers I realized not only would I not be able to afford to buy a house, but I wouldn't even be able to afford rent. I realized I would have to move back in with my parents if I wanted to survive. That is real motivation to continue going to college and get a better job. Not that I don't love my parents or anything; it would just be better not to live with them.

19) I learned that I probably chose to date the only guy on campus who has commitment issues.

20) I learned that Professor Howard is older than I thought. I found out that he taught my father something like a million years ago.

21) Liking math won't kill you. Many people think that hating math is cool, but in reality it isn't.

22) I never knew there was a kind of math class like this. I learned that math is often a common sense class, in which I can base a judgement off of that intuition. Of course, I also learned that I think things that aren't correct because I sometimes lack common sense.

23) I have learned that if I have low expectations in life I am happier because I can be pleasantly surprised instead of painfully disappointed. It took a couple of tests for me to figure this out, but I did.

Scouts, Pickups, and Sprinklers

My scouts were adamant about wanting to ride in the back of my pickup, and Gordy was their spokesman. "Riding in the front of a pickup is stupid," he said. "Riding in the back is awesome."

I have always felt that when it comes to working with scouts, a person has to pick his battles. Some battles truly are worth fighting head-on. For others, an alternate way should be found. Then there are those that should not be fought at all. I found this to be a good philosophy, especially in my case with the eighteen boys in my troop. They were hard-working farm boys, and there were certain things they would really dig in their heels about.

I had always felt that riding in the back of a pickup wasn't safe. However, when I was scoutmaster, there was no rule against it, so I knew that particular battle would be one based solely on my own opinion.

With all of these ideas in mind, I took some time to consider my options before I answered. As I was thinking, Gordy tried to strengthen their position. "We've been working so hard that we really need a chance to cool off."

I had to admit that the boys had worked hard. We had done a service project, mowing and raking all of the widows' lawns in the community. Though the boys were quite typical and did lots of crazy things while we worked, they had also done a good job.

Finally, taking everything into account, I decided I would let them ride in the back, on the condition that they sat down in the bottom of the pickup. I also told them that I would drive slower. They agreed to that, even though they were anxious to get back to the church to play basketball.

The boys packed into the back of my pickup, stuffing their rakes under their feet. We started down the road at about thirty miles per hour. Then I saw something that I thought might help the boys reconsider the joy of riding in the back of a pickup. It was a huge center pivot sprinkler with a high-volume end gun that was putting out gallons of water every second. I could see the huge stream of water booming out like a water cannon, and it was moving toward the road. I slowed my pickup to synchronize it to the distance and speed of the sprinkler.

The boys didn't see the sprinkler. They had only one thing on their mind, and that was basketball.

"What's the matter?" Gordy yelled. "Won't this pickup go any faster?"

"You need to get a Chevy," Mort said.

"A Chevy?" Devon questioned. "If it were a Chevy it would be dead in the road, and we wouldn't be going any . . . "

Devon didn't even finish before the water hit them with the force of a fire hose, and in seconds it dumped tens of gallons of water over them. Even as they hollered I slowed my speed to about five miles per hour, matching the turning speed of the sprinkler. I worked the gas, brake, and clutch, making the pickup stutter, lurch, and finally come to a complete stop just as the back of the pickup finished filling with water and the sprinkler turned away from the road.

Through all of the screaming, Gordy yelled, "What the devil was that all about?"

"You guys are right," I answered. "I need to get a new pickup that doesn't stall out in water."

"Yeah, right," Gordy said sarcastically.

I started the pickup back up, and we headed on our way. And, can you believe it, there was another sprinkler that hit the road just as we went by with the exact same experience, except that the boys saw it coming this time and were hollering even before it hit them. And I don't know if you believe in coincidences, but we even had an unimaginable third one hit us before we finally arrived at the church.

When we pulled into the church parking lot, the water was still draining from the pickup. I opened the tailgate and water poured out as if I was opening a floodgate. I smiled as the boys slogged out and tried to dry off so they could go inside to play basketball.

"I guess that is a chance you take when you ride in the back of a pickup," I said, smiling.

"Or the chance we take when we have an idiot driver," Gordy growled.

The Wrong Kind of Gas

Only two miles from where I grew up was a dude ranch called "The Fun Farm." There, overlooking the river, were nice campsites with fire pits and limited amenities. Each day there were activities offered to the campers. For an extra fee, a person could go on a horse ride or go river rafting. For no cost a person was allowed to go into the barn and watch cows being milked, help feed calves, or gather eggs.

It just happened that the campground was also by the bridge where we teenagers gathered each evening. After a hard day of hauling hay, changing pipe, milking cows, and countless other types of work, we would meet there for a refreshing swim.

Although the campground was right beside the bridge, we seldom had any contact with the campers. They kept to themselves, and so did we. But one summer, a man named Jim, who was camping at the campground, came over and asked if he could join us. We didn't have a problem with that, and soon he was coming every night.

Most campers don't stay for more than a week, so after he had come swimming with us for most of a month, we asked him about it.

"Oh," Jim said, "I have a government job working in this area for the summer. It's just as cheap for me to stay here in a camper as it is to get an apartment, and I can enjoy the river and the country more."

"But I would think after a while it would get tiring living in a motorhome," I said.

"Well," he replied, "there is one thing that has really been annoying. I do wish they had septic connects at the camp sites. The septic tank on my motor home is really small. Every few days I have to put up my awning and all of that and drive to town to the dump station. In addition, my motorhome is getting horrible gas mileage.

I seem to only be getting a few miles to the gallon because I have to fill up almost every time I drive it. "

"There is something you could do," Lenny said. "Most of those motorhomes have two gas tanks. One guy I know changed one of his gas tanks to a septic tank. He said he didn't travel enough to need that much gas."

Jim became excited about this. He asked if we knew someone who could do the conversion. We told him that there was a man who did camper and motorhome work who lived only a couple of miles away.

We didn't see Jim for a few days because he had to stay in a hotel while his motorhome was retrofitted. But it wasn't very long before he came back to join us for a swim.

After a couple more days, Lenny asked, "So how's the camping now?"

"It seems to be working well," Jim replied. "I have been watching my tank meter, and if it is indicating the level correctly, I should have enough capacity now to last more than a week at a time." He then smiled broadly. "In addition, I think the retrofit has solved my low gas mileage problem."

"How's that?" I asked.

"Well, late last night I heard some noise outside my motorhome, and I went to investigate. There was a gas siphon hose sticking out of my new septic tank. Apparently, the would-be thief had sucked on it to siphon out gas and got a little more than he bargained for. He had thrown up all over the ground."

Lenny laughed. "It sounds like he got the wrong kind of gas in his tank."

A Flood of Procrastination

I was just leaving my office at the university when the hail hit. It was the size of marbles, and it really hurt. I raced for my van. Once inside, the hail fell so hard I thought it was going to break the windows. It did leave some small dents in the roof.

As I started on my way, the hail changed to rain that came down as if someone was pouring a giant bucket of water out of the sky. Before I had gone half a mile, the water was so deep in the streets that it was nearly up to the door of my van. Yet only a couple of miles further, there was not a drop of rain at all. The storm dropped a couple of inches of rain in only an hour or two, but its path was only about three miles wide.

The university town where I work was probably hit the hardest. Water running down the hill flowed into campus buildings, apartments, and houses all over town. When the rain stopped, everyone moved quickly to help each other.

The next day, class work was nearly impossible, as everyone had a tale to tell. David said his apartment was on a second floor and untouched, so he had set out to help others. He organized a group of boys who went to apartments that had basement stairwells. He would yell to the apartment tenants, "Don't open your door until we bucket out the stairwell."

At the first two apartments, the tenants opened their doors and asked, "What?" The water then flooded in. After that, he would wade waste deep into the sewage-filled water and hold the doorknob until the occupants of the apartment understood his request. Then he and the other boys would work quickly to empty the stairwell. Many good deeds were performed and the damage was far less than it could have been.

But Tanya didn't have a happy story to tell. In fact, she was the opposite of happy. "I had been driving into Rexburg when the storm hit," she said. "The water came so fast that my car started to stutter and to stall. I hoped I could keep it running until I made it up the hill to my apartment. When I came to the roundabout, I had to stop — not for another car, but for an idiot who was paddling a kayak around and around it, and wasn't even signaling."

"I don't think kayaks have signals," I replied.

"Well, I just about ran over the moron," she said. "And when I finally got past the roundabout and headed up the hill, here came a whole gang of stupid people sailing down the flooded street on inner tubes. I tried to dodge them and finally stopped, but they were totally out of control and banged into my car and everything. Then I couldn't get my car going again and had to leave it until later."

When she finished, John raised his hand. When I called on him, he was all smiles. "Well," he said, "I think that the flood was an answer to my prayers."

"It has been awful dry," I answered, "and we definitely needed rain, but I wouldn't say we needed that much rain."

"Oh, I wasn't thinking about that at all," he replied. "I hadn't had time to study for your test, and I was sure I would fail it. But since it was closing last night, I had to take it anyway. I was in line at the testing center waiting to get in when the water started swirling around my ankles. The test center people yelled for everyone to leave, saying our teachers would have to make allowances for us. And now that you have had to open the test for a couple more days, I have time to study."

Two days later, after the test had closed, we met again for class. I asked, "So, John, did you ace the test with the two extra days to study?"

John rolled his eyes. "No. God answered my prayer for more time to study by flooding the whole campus, and I still failed. But I learned something even more important."

"What?" I asked.

"I learned that no matter how much time I have, I will always find ways to procrastinate until it's gone."

Every summer, many of the different church congregations and small communities form youth softball teams for a big tournament. It is a big event. But the year when I was fourteen, there was an abundance of young men in my small, rural community. The older boys decided that they didn't want us younger boys playing with them.

"You insist that everyone gets to play," David, the leader of the older boys, said to the community leaders. "The younger boys are no good and will just make us lose. They can form their own team."

Our community leaders didn't like it but finally gave in. "Pa" was the name we affectionately called the old man who had always coached us. The older boys asked Pa to coach them, but he shook his head. "I think the younger boys are the ones who need me."

The community leaders still expected the older boys, who were called team A, to practice with us younger boys, who were called team B. But again, the older boys refused. "We can't improve our skills practicing against a team that isn't any good," David said.

The older boys also told all of the other teams in the community how bad we were, and no one else would practice with us, either. But then Pa received a call from the J.C.C., the Juvenile Correction Center. Though the state rules would not allow the boys there to leave to compete in the big tournament, they had formed a team and hoped the other teams in the community would come there to play. But none of the other teams would. David and the older boys even went so far as to say that they were sure the J.C.C. team couldn't be any good, and it would be degrading for any team to go there.

Pa asked us if we would play the J.C.C team. We accepted, excited to have a team to play against, even though we wondered what they would be like.

We soon learned that it was an earned privilege for a boy there to get to play, so they were stellar examples of sportsmanship. We also learned that they were superb ball players, far superior to many in our region. On our first matchup with them, we had a humiliating loss of 50 to nothing, and only 50 because they quit counting there.

But as the summer progressed, and we played against them night after night, they were kind to teach us, and we saw our skill markedly improving. By the time we played our last game against them, they only beat us 7 to 5.

The big summer tournament opened with our team matched against one of the best teams. When we handily beat them, all of the other teams in the area took notice. Our A team lost their first game, and we advanced to play the team that beat them.

They not only laughed and mocked us, telling us we would lose to any team that beat them, but they came to cheer for our opponents. Pa was so angry he could hardly contain himself. But when we beat that team as well, and we felt like gloating back against the older boys, Pa reminded us of the sportsmanship we had learned from the J.C.C. boys.

"There are some things that are even more important than winning," he said.

To the shock of almost everyone, we made it to the championship game. The older boys from our A team came dressed to play.

"What do you think you're doing?" Pa asked.

"It's our community team that is playing, so we came to play," David said. "We will help them out."

"You can help them out by getting off the field," Pa said. "You are not part of this team."

The older boys were angry, and they again joined the cheering section of our opponents. It was a hard fought game, and we lost 7 to 6. As the older boys from our community cheered our loss, Pa reminded us to keep our composure and congratulate our opponents on their win.

After awarding the winning team their trophy, the tournament director called our team over. "For the prize of honor in clean play, good values, and, I might add, not judging others, I am pleased to award this team the sportsmanship trophy," he said.

When he handed us the trophy, I read the plaque on it, and it said, "No prize exceeds the honor one brings to himself by treating others well."

Where Everyone Knows You

As my wife, Donna, and I were dating and were trying to learn more about each other, we talked about what we desired from life. Our differences quickly became apparent. She grew up in Los Angeles, and I grew up in the middle of nowhere.

When I asked her where she wanted to live, she said, "Tahiti would be nice."

This was because she had come to Idaho for college and had endured one of our winters. However, she said she would settle for anywhere a few degrees south of freezing to death.

"What about the size of the town?" I asked. That, to me, was the most important thing.

"What difference does that make?" she replied.

"What difference does that make?" I repeated in surprise. "Why, that makes all the difference in the world!"

When I was growing up, our nearest neighbor was almost a mile away. I knew every person that lived within a ten-mile radius of us (all ten of them). On the other hand, when I went to visit her family for the first time, she hardly knew the name of a single person who lived on her block.

I learned that quickly. When we arrived at her parents' house, the first thing we did was to go inside so I could meet her family. Then I went out to the car to unload our luggage. Not far away I saw a neighbor who was watering his lawn. I thought I would be friendly, so I went over to say hello. I introduced myself and told him I was a friend of Donna's family.

"Who?" he asked.

I pointed to Donna's parents' home. "Your neighbors, the Walkers."

"Oh, is that the name of the people who live there?" he replied.

I thought he might be new in the neighborhood, but I found out he had lived there for forty years. I continued trying to visit, but he just looked at me strangely. Eventually, he went inside and peered suspiciously at me through the curtains.

So when Donna asked me where I wanted to live, I knew exactly what to say.

"I want to live in a place where the population is small enough that if someone addresses a letter to me and all they put on the envelope is my name, the town, the state, and the zip, I will still get it."

She laughed. "That is impossible. You know very well that won't happen anywhere."

I couldn't convince her that I felt it would. Nonetheless, despite our major differences, we married. We spent many years with my going to college and finally returned to live in Idaho in a very small, rural community.

Then came the day that I started writing short stories. Over the years my stories have gradually reached a wider and wider audience through hundreds of newspapers and magazines across the U.S., Canada, and other parts of the world. A few of my stories have even run in magazines with millions of readers.

One day, after one of my stories ran in one of those magazines, I came home to a surprise. As I walked in the door, Donna handed me a letter. It was from a lady who said she was an older woman who enjoyed one of my stories immensely. She told me a bit about her life and why my stories meant so much to her. It was a lot of fun to read.

After I finished reading it, I read it to Donna, and she smiled. "That is all wonderful, but there is something more important. Look at the address."

"Yes, I can see she is from Pennsylvania."

"Not her address," Donna said. "Yours."

I looked at the address, and it had nothing more than my name, the town, state, and zip code, and yet it had still been delivered.

I smiled and knew that I had found the home I had wanted.

Forgiveness

Isaac's little four-year-old granddaughter came running to him, filthy from toe to brow. He pulled her onto his lap and wiped some mud from her face. Her beautiful blond hair was so full of dirt that it looked almost brown.

"Grandpa, me make mud pies," she said.

In an instant, he felt tears coming to his eyes. His little granddaughter's voice, her filthy appearance, and the mention of mud pies all combined to bring back a memory with such force that he wasn't prepared for it.

He had lived in a small town in France at the time of Hitler's army's invasion. The men of the whole region quickly formed an underground resistance to the German army. They did whatever they could to thwart the Germans' efforts. During one of their missions to destroy some of the enemies supplies, some German soldiers had been killed.

The German commanding officer decided to take revenge and chose Isaac's hometown to pay the price. While Isaac and other men were away helping with the resistance, they got the word. He and the other men of his town rushed home. They learned from the few survivors that the women and children had gathered in the church where they had thought they would be safe. The men and boys who were still left in the town were rounded up by the Germans and gunned down in the town square. Then the Germans blocked the doors of the church and burned it to the ground with the women and children inside.

Isaac found out that his wife and his children had all been killed. He had felt a hatred build in him that ate at his whole being. He felt a desire for revenge to kill every German he could find. He and the men who had lost their families joined the Allied army that landed at Normandy, and they fought to push the Germans out of France and then continued fighting on across Europe.

The men who had lost their families were ferocious fighters.

Because they had no one to return home to, they fearlessly risked their lives at every turn. As the war wound down and they marched into Berlin, Isaac wondered what he would do with his life when the war was over because all he lived for was vengeance on his enemies.

Then, one day, he saw a little four-year-old German girl. She was thin and filthy and looked to be making mud pies. But after she finished making them, she started to eat them, and he realized how hungry she was.

That night, as he was eating his small rations, he set them down for just a moment and someone grabbed them. With lightning reflexes, Isaac grabbed the person's wrist and turned to look at the would-be thief. In the dimming light, he saw the blond hair of a German, and that was all he needed. He pulled out his revolver. But as he raised it, the fearful cry of a child caused him to look deeper, and he realized it was the same girl he had seen earlier.

As he gazed into her frightened eyes, he thought of his own little daughter. At the time his daughter had been killed, she had been about the age of this little girl. The anger and hatred raged in him and fought against feelings of tenderness for this child. But finally, the slightest bit of compassion emerged in his heart. As he continued to hold her wrist to keep her from fleeing, he put his gun away and reached for the food she had dropped. He picked it up and held it out to her. She carefully took it, and when he let go of her, she darted away, taking the food with her.

For the first time, he thought about what he was doing, and felt the unmistakable understanding that two wrongs do not make a right. Destroying others for having had his own family killed would not bring them back.

He realized that if he was ever to find any peace in his life, he was going to have to learn to forgive.

An Understanding of Innocence

Isaac's oldest sons had been shot by the Germans. His wife
and younger children had gathered with others in a church for safety,
only to have the Germans block the doors and burn the church down.
Isaac joined the war with revenge being his only desire. But after
the Allies had taken Berlin, he came across a four-year-old German
girl who was starving. Without thinking, he had pulled his revolver
and nearly shot her when she attempted to steal food from him. But
then he had found a small bit of compassion in his heart and not only
let her go, but shared what little he had.

He never expected to see her again, but the next day she
came. He could see in her face how hungry she was, but his rations
were barely enough for himself. He struggled with thoughts that it
was those like her who had killed his family. But then, in the next
instant, he could see in her his own small daughter who had died in
the fire.

Finally, after the battle had raged in his heart for some time,
he divided his food and held out half of it to her. She cautiously
crept closer. Once she reached him, she took the food and darted
away.

Each evening after that she grew more confident, and would
come closer. Soon she didn't flee so quickly. Then, one day, before
their usual meal time, he heard a cry and turned to see her running
toward him. Two men were chasing her with less than honorable
intent. Isaac had grown accustomed to the horrors and ravishes of
war, even of the very young, but this still sickened him. Even
though the men were on the same side of the war as he was, Isaac
felt anger swell in him. The girl ran behind Isaac and hugged his
waist in fear. Isaac pulled his gun and faced the men. The men
could see the angered expression on his face and quickly backed

away.

The girl still held onto him, her face buried against him. Then Isaac did something he thought he could never do; he leaned down and hugged this little girl. That night, as he shared his food with her, she did not flee away but stayed close. After they had eaten, Isaac did the best he could to help her understand that he would walk her safely home.

When they arrived at the place she indicated she lived, Isaac saw it was nothing but a bombed-out building. He looked for an adult and finally found an old woman. Through her broken French and his limited German, he was able to learn about the little girl. Isaac found out that her name was Alexandra and that she had no family. Her father, a German soldier, had been killed while fighting. The rest of her family had been killed as the battle moved into Berlin.

Isaac suddenly felt a surge of anger. What if the girl's father had been part of those who had killed his family? Then another thought came. What if, as he himself had been fighting, he had been the one who had killed her father or others of her family? He started to think about how Alexandra had done nothing wrong. There were many on both sides who didn't want to fight but had no choice. It is usually the innocent who pay the biggest price in any conflict.

The old lady watched Alexandra and could see the trust she had in Isaac. "Do you have family?" the lady asked him.

"They were all killed by the Germans," Isaac said quietly. "One was a daughter Alexandra's age."

The lady was silent for a moment, and when she spoke, she spoke with great empathy. "You have lost your family, and so has she. Perhaps she was brought to you, and you to her, because you need each other so that you can both have a family once more."

As Isaac considered this, the lady spoke again. "I cannot take care of her. If she stays here, she will most likely die."

Isaac wondered if he could find the forgiveness in his heart to raise a child of the enemy that had killed his family. And if he did, could he love her as his own daughter?

As he looked at Alexandra and she looked up at him with her trusting big blue eyes, he determined it would be worth it to try.

A Change of Heart

Isaac's family had been brutally murdered by the Germans, and he had joined the war with revenge being his only desire. But after Berlin fell to the Allies, he found some compassion for a starving four-year-old German girl who tried to steal food from him. The old lady at the bombed-out building where the little girl lived told him the girl's name was Alexandra and that her family had all been killed. The old lady suggested he take the little girl as his own, saying otherwise she would likely die.

At first Isaac balked at the idea of raising a child of the enemy who had killed his family. But he realized he needed Alexandra as much as she needed him and that she was innocent of the atrocities that the war had created around her.

Because the old lady spoke little French and he spoke little German, communicating was hard. Eventually he was able to get her to understand that he wanted her to ask Alexandra if she would like to be his daughter. When she did, Alexandra pointed at him and then to her own mouth, and he understood that she was asking if he would feed her. He smiled and nodded. She ran to him and threw her arms around his waist, and he realized how much she had grown to trust him. In return, he felt a warm, almost imperceptible feeling of love in his heart that was starting to burn away the stone-cold hate.

He took Alexandra back to his camp. He didn't know how he was going to manage getting her back to France, but he knew he was not going to leave her behind. He had her stay at his tent, and he approached his commanding officer.

"Captain, I have a request."

"Yes, Sergeant, what is it?"

"There is a little four-year-old girl that . . . "

The captain didn't even let him finish. "Is this the one that you have been sharing your food with?"

Isaac was surprised. "You've seen her?"

The captain nodded. "Not only that, but I saw you protect her from the men who planned to harm her today. I was surprised that you, of all people, could feel any kindness for a German."

"She's just a child, Sir. I took her back to her home, but I found out she has no family. An old lady there said she would likely die if no one looks after her. I would like that chance."

The captain spoke sternly. "I find that surprising. You, of all people, with your hatred from the loss of your family. I thought you could never find forgiveness. And just how do you plan to get her back to your home in France?"

"I was hoping you could provide some written order for her to be able to board the train with me," Isaac replied. "If not, I will walk the whole way, if I have to, in order to take her."

The captain was silent for a moment. Finally, he nodded. "You know, as I see it, everyone in her immediate family is dead, and you are just escorting her to find other distant family members."

"But she doesn't have any other . . . "

The captain held up his hand. "Are you not planning to be her family? And do you not live a distance away?"

Isaac suddenly understood and smiled. "Yes, Sir."

"I will have the company clerk draw up the papers for you to be her escort," the Captain said, "along with your official release papers."

"Thank you, Sir," Isaac replied.

"I can help you with the military clearance," the captain said. "But I cannot authorize any extra food. I'm afraid you will have to do whatever you can for that."

"I will continue to share my rations with her, Sir."

"That is hardly enough for one, let alone two."

"We'll make do."

And with that, Isaac prepared willingly to face what would likely be a challenging journey, but he did so with a renewed purpose, and a small feeling of love beginning to grow in his heart.

Sacrifice and Forgiveness

Isaac's family had been brutally murdered by the Germans, and he had joined the war with revenge being his only desire. But after Berlin fell to the Allies, he grew fond of a four-year-old German girl, Alexandra, who an old lady said would likely die if no one took care of her. His commanding officer was kind enough to provide papers indicating that her family had died and Isaac was escorting her to "other" family on his way home from the war. The "other" family was to be Isaac, and he knew that even with the papers the journey could be perilous.

When he boarded the train for his home in France, he was viewed with great suspicion. Alexandra, with her blond hair and blue eyes, was clearly German. The army officials double-checked his release and escort papers. Finally, the officials left them alone, and the train started to move.

Isaac shared what little food he had with her. He hoped it would be clear sailing all the way to France, but each time the train stopped, he was questioned again with greater intensity. At one point, Alexandra was almost taken away, and he was nearly arrested. That was when Isaac realized that when they reached the border, it would be worse. But he was not about to give her up.

At the next stop, he took her and they quickly disembarked. He figured it would be safer to cross into France on foot. It was at least twenty miles to the border and then hundreds of miles to his home. As they walked, Alexandra never complained, but when she started to stumble, he knew she was tired.

Isaac put his pack around Alexandra and then lifted her onto his shoulders. He scrounged up a little food as they went along, and he knew she was still hungry, but she was always appreciative of whatever he gave her.

As they approached the boarder, Isaac could see it was heavily guarded. He moved carefully along it, staying under cover as much as possible, until he found a unit that bore the French insignia. As he tried to make his way across the border, he and Alexandra were quickly surrounded. He showed his papers and explained what he was doing, but their animosity toward the enemy showed in their feelings toward Alexandra. Isaac eventually procured their passage by surrendering the cigarettes from his rations he had saved for just such an emergency.

They still had a long way to go, and the nights were often cold. He had only one blanket, which he gave to her, and she would still snuggle close to him to stay warm. As they walked day after day, people sometimes shared food, and sometimes he would exchange work for something to eat. But he found out that if the people saw Alexandra, they usually refused his request.

This made him examine his own heart. He thought about how he had nearly shot her when she had first stolen food from him. Yet now he would give his life to protect her. He knew the prejudice and the hate that others showed had also once been in his heart. That helped him be more forgiving of them.

When they finally arrived at his hometown, there were few people left. The Germans had killed almost everyone. He found the greatest prejudice of all there. He was ostracized and despised because he had chosen to adopt Alexandra as his own daughter. He had to always protect her. But thankfully, as the years passed, memories grew dim, and the animosity faded away.

Now, as he pulled his little four-year-old granddaughter onto his lap and wiped away the mud, he smiled. With her blond hair and blue eyes, she was the very image of the little girl he had rescued so many years before. He shuddered at the thought of his intentions when he had drawn his pistol that day Alexandra first stole food from him. He thought of how hard it was at that time to find forgiveness in his heart for the massacre of his family. He thought of the trials he had faced to save her. But when his little granddaughter looked up, smiled, and said, "Gampa, I love you," he knew he had been paid back a hundredfold.

But mostly, he knew that the forgiveness he had found in his heart and the sacrifice he had given had all been worth it.

If you enjoyed our book, we would love to have you do a review on Amazon at:
http://amzn.com/1629860069

Would you like to see Life's Outtakes column running in your local paper or magazine? Suggest it to the editor. If an editor runs the Life's Outtakes column due to your suggestion, we will send you one of Daris Howard's books, of your choice, signed by the author. Find out more at:
http://www.darishoward.com

Read other stories, purchase more books, or sign up for a short story each week by going to
http://www.publishinginspiration.com

Other books
by
Daris Howard
Daris Howard Amazon page:
http://amzn.com/e/B004H76UGK

For inspiring plays and books, as well as discounts for book sellers, go to

http://www.publishinginspiration.com

About The Author

Daris Howard is an author and playwright who grew up on a farm in rural Idaho. He associated with many colorful characters including cowboys, farmers, lumberjacks and others. Besides his work on the farm he has worked as a cowboy and a mechanic. He was a state champion athlete and competed in college athletics. He also lived for eighteen months in New York.

Daris and his wife, Donna, have ten children and were foster parents for several years. He has also worked in scouting and cub scouts, at one time having eighteen boys in his scout troop.

His plays, musicals, and books build on the characters of those he has associated with, along with his many experiences, to bring his work to life.

Daris is a math professor and his classes are well known for the stories he tells to liven up discussion and to help bring across the points he is trying to teach. His scripts and books are much like his stories, full of humor and inspiration.

He and his family have enjoyed running a summer community theatre where he had a chance to premiere his theatrical works and rework them to make them better. His published plays and books can be seen at http://www.darishoward.com. He has plays translated into German and French and his works have been done in many countries around the world.

In the last years, Daris has started writing books and short stories. He writes a popular news column called *Life's Outtakes*, that consists of weekly short stories and is published in various newspapers and magazines in the United States and Canada, including *Country*, *Horizons*, and *Family Living*.

www.ingramcontent.com/pod-product-compliance
Lightning Source LLC
Chambersburg PA
CBHW060629130626
46555CB00002B/724